INQUIRIES & ADVERTISING

Address: Suite 22, 509 Commissioners Road West, London, Ontario, N6J 1Y5

Advertising: Email info@mysterymagazine.ca

Editor: Kerry Carter **Publisher:** Chuck Carter **Cover Artist:** Robin Grenville Evans

Submissions: https://mysterymagazine.ca/submit.asp

CAJUN STATE

O'Neil De Noux

I've never seen Chief Marcus Boone so shook up. He gives me a withered look from behind his desk, wipes sweat from his brow and says, "This is bad. Real bad."

It's barely six a.m., December nineteenth and we are in the university police station, me sitting in one of the cushioned chairs in front of the chief's desk, the chief in his captain's chair behind the desk. Marcus's eyes are red-rimmed and he looks … old, his dark blue uniform shirt seems two sizes too big as he yanks his collar, ala Rodney Dangerfield. He's small to begin with, topping off at five-five, while I stand six-two. At forty-four, I'm ten years younger.

I wait, as good cops do, for him to continue. Complainants, as well as chiefs of police, restart conversations automatically. After popping a second stick of nicotine gum into his mouth, he says, "They stole our Christmas tree last night."

"What Christmas tree?"

The chief's eyes bulge as if I'd just blasphemed.

"The *big* tree. The one in the middle of Frenchmen's Circle. Between Evangeline Oaks."

OK, a little background information is due at this point. My name is Hunter Bourget, born and raised in New Orleans, a product of St. Anthony of Padua Grammar School and Archangel High School, graduate of Loyola University with a degree in Criminology and a graduate of the New Orleans Police Academy, retired from NOPD after twenty-two years, the last nine as a homicide detective. I've been working here at Cajun State University in Abbeville, Louisiana, for three months. Although I've a French last name, I'm not Cajun. My grandfather came from France after World War I.

When Marcus, who'd been my lieutenant at NOPD, brought me out for an interview back in August, he'd declared, "Man-o-man. You gotta come here. This is the perfect retirement job." So one month after retiring from NOPD, getting the hell out of the big city, I took the new position as a police investigator with the university police, got my state commission, gold Louisiana badge, a new desk and a campus map. They'd showed me Evangeline Oaks, my first day on the job. I remember huge, moss-draped live oaks I still not sure where they are on campus. That's why I have a map.

"Any leads?" I ask.

Marcus shakes his head. "We didn't even know it was stolen until five a.m., when one of the science professors monitoring an experiment in the lab building noticed. We got broken ornaments all over the ground, half a string of lights, drag marks across the circle. Damn tree was twenty feet tall. They musta had a truck." He waved his arms. "Big ole truck just parks by the circle and they load up the tree and roll off campus and none of our patrol officers see a damn thing."

When I was NOPD, my first training officer taught me, no matter what you do on the midnight shift, before you knock off—you ride your beat to see if anything's amiss. Better for the police to 'just miss' something than a civilian to call in and say, 'remember the statue of Joan of Arc in the middle of Decatur Street, the one that's been there for about a hundred years? Well it was there last night, and it's gone now.'

A tap at the door turns me around as one of our sergeants, the big one, the one they call Shrek because he looks like … well, Shrek, steps in. I glance at his name tag as he enters. Russian name—Komarovsky. I remember now. Been meaning to ask if he's related to the guy in Dr. Zhivago, the guy played by Rod Steiger.

Komarovsky gives me a meek look—not easy when you look like a comic version of The Incredible Hulk. He plants himself, back against the wall and tells the chief, "Got the trip sheets for you. We patrolled Frenchmen's Circle at twelve-thirty, two a.m., three-twenty, four-fifteen and five o'clock."

"Five? He didn't see the tree was missing but the damn professor noticed. Who drove by at five?"

"Simmons?"

"He blind, or what?"

Komarovsky shrugs and looks at me. "I'm snake bit, you know."

"Not really."

"Everything goes wrong when it's my shift."

"You weren't bitten by a snake," the chief growls. "You were born under the sign of the vulture."

Vulture? I heard of Pisces, you know, the fish and if I can recall what the name of the crab is, I'll die a happy man.

"You got anything more for me?" the chief asks Komarovsky.

"Not really."

Marcus lets out a long sigh and waves Komarovsky away. "Try not to lose a building tomorrow night." He leans forward, elbows on the desk and tells me, "You know what to do. You solved enough murders. Find out who took our tree." He closes his eyes and adds, "I gotta call the VPHD." That's Cajun State UPD lingo for the Vice-President we answer to—Vice-President in Charge of Human Development. We develop no inhumans here at Cajun State University.

I try to get out, but before I can make a clean getaway, he calls out, "Spare no expense."

"I have an expense account?"

"You know what I mean." He waves his hands in the air again. "Turn over every rock, look in every cranny. Call out the cavalry if you need them!"

The only rocks we have on campus are around the big fountain over by the science building, at least I think it's the science building. Could be Literature. I almost bump into Komarovsky in the hall and ask him, "We have crannies around here?"

"What?"

"Never mind."

The phone in my tiny office is ringing. It's the chief who says, "Call the feds. I'm serious."

"Any particular feds?"

"All of 'em." He hangs up.

I pour myself a fresh cup of coffee-and-chicory, put in a dollop of half-and-half and two Equals, sit behind my desk and flip through the incident report on the stolen tree. Isn't much to it. Initial call came in at 0505 hours, our unit arrived at 0508 hours only to describe the scene. Our other two marked police cars searched the area to no avail. Only person spoken to was the professor who'd called in and all he saw was an empty spot where the tree used to stand. It was a spruce. No distinguishing scars, marks or tattoos, only about four hundred dollars of ornaments and lights, including a white angel atop.

Komarovsky passes down the hall again and I call out, "Which of our frats is most likely to pull a stunt like this?"

He leans against the door frame. "All of them. They pull pranks all the time, like filling plastic Gatorade bottles with dry ice, drop in a little water and tossing them off the balconies to the parking lots. Sounds like a bomb going off. They keep hot-wiring the washers and dryers on the weekend so everyone gets to do their laundry free."

"Panty raids?" I ask as I take a sip of coffee.

"Most of the girls here don't wear panties."

OK. Too much info. I offer him some coffee but he just shakes his head and wanders off. I reach into my desk drawer and pull out the phone book. The nearest

FBI office is the resident agent in Lake Charles. He answers after the third ring and hangs up on me after my fourth sentence. Obviously I'm a crank caller, reporting to the top law enforcement agency in the nation that our spruce was purloined.

My subsequent calls to DEA and ICE in New Orleans are cut off in mid-conversation. How did Tommy Lee Jones put it in the movie *Men in Black?* "We have no sense of humor we're aware of." Feds.

I turn to my iMac—I'm the only one on the department who uses a Macintosh, my own of course, because once you use a Mac there's no going back to driving a stick shift—and start searching for the web sites of the Royal Canadian Mounted Police in Montreal; the Sureté in Paris; Scotland Yard in London; Interpol in St. Cloud, France; the Ghana Police Service because I can't ignore the entire continent of Africa; the Federal Police in Rio de Janeiro, Brazil; the Federales in Mexico City; the city Militia in Moscow, Russia; the Tokyo Metropolitan Police, the Delhi Police in India; the Perth Police Constabulary in Australia; the Carabinieri and Questura in Rome; as well as the Swiss Guard in the Vatican. Fifteen emails later, it's time to call the Abbeville City Police.

Captain Duplantier Jeanfreau confirms what I suspect. There has been a rash of Christmas decoration thefts in the small town and in surrounding inhabited areas of Vermilion Parish, where Cajun State University lies. Pretty hard to have Christmas decorations stolen from uninhabited areas of the parish, but I don't mention that.

On my way to lunch at the campus café, I run into Adrien Jones, my first victim, a sophomore. He'd been cyberstalked by his old girlfriend and cyberstalking is a serious crime in Louisiana. OK, maybe not that serious but serious enough.

"So, heard from any old girlfriends lately?" I ask Adrien as we both walk toward the café.

"Not since you slapped the handcuffs on Lucy"

Lucy Gros was pretty, damn pretty, which made me glad I wasn't twenty years younger because I could get in trouble here. No, I didn't slap my cuffs on her, didn't even arrest her, I just gave her a summons to go to court and let the judge hash it out.

"Did you hear anything about our missing Christmas tree?"

"What tree?"

"The one in the middle of Frenchmen's Circle. Between Evangeline Oaks."

"We have a Christmas tree there?"

"Had. Someone stole it."

Adrien is short and wiry with a straight brown hair cut like Moe Howard (as in the Three Stooges). He laughs aloud and I chuckle along with him momentarily, then turn serious.

"Seriously," I say. "If you hear anything, I'd appreciate a call."

Just as we enter the café, he says, "Y'all seen that old movie *Animal House?*"

Jesus, I remember when John Belushi was alive and well. Maybe not well, but alive. "Yes," I tell him. I've seen the movie maybe twenty times.

"We don't have a Delta House here but we got frats that raise Armadillos to race and try to tame cottonmouths." Racing Armadillos?

As we enter the café, the clatter of trays and silverware echoes and the smell of fried cooking fills the air. "How the hell do you tame a cottonmouth?" I have to ask.

" 'Zactly," Adrien says and eases away from me.

After an unhealthy, but tasty meal of fried catfish, hush puppies (those not from the South need to know—no it's not dog meat or puppy chow, it's deep-fried cornbread), steamed okra, washed down by sweet tea (we pre-sweeten it down here)—I make the rounds of the frat houses on and off campus.

Returning to my office just before four p.m., I have to admit I was surprised at the cooperation and friendliness of the fraternities. Hell, they got a good laugh, every one, when I told them about the stolen tree. The consensus was—why didn't we think of it?

The chief steps in just as I boot up my iMac. He looks even more hangdog than earlier as he leans in the doorway and says, "Got anything for me?"

I tell him about the feds and the frats as I access my email then go over them with him. Only three responses so far. Inspector O. Watanabe of The Tokyo Metropolitan Police respectfully replied he has no information, then asks if we had a specific lead pointing to Japan. Detective C. Almodiovar of the Federal Police in Rio de Janeiro, Brazil, asks if we have any professors on campus who spoke Portuguese who could send the email in Portuguese since their translators seem to think I'm searching for, of all things, a tree.

I got the following reply from Commander A.R. Pith-Martin, Chief Constable of the Perth Police Constabulary in Australia, "What the hell is this about, matey? A freaking tree? Are you a lunatic or what?"

"Man should be suspended," the chief snarls as he leaves.

I print copies of all my emails and responses because I've already learned—here in college, you keep a paper trail because every dean and vice-president (and we have more vice-presidents than a South American banana republic has generals) has a right to read our reports and boy, do they ever.

The next morning I discover the Italian Questura has a sense of humor, at least Sergeant I.M. Golosini does. His email reads, "It is upsetting to have your Christmas icon stolen. I have made immediate inquiries and learned a perhaps stolen tree is being used as a model for art students at the Michelangelo Academy of Art in Florence. We have a man checking this out. Please you could better explain what state is the state called Cajun. I have been to New York twice and have a map of USA but unable to find a state called Cajun among the fifty states of USA."

The email continues, "Our man in Florence just reported to me as I sit here at the computer, the tree used in Florence is a northern pine and your missing icon is a spruce. Alas, we are of no help. But we will continue to look into the matter."

I fire up a pot of coffee-and-chicory and try my best to explain the state called Cajun in my response.

"Dear Sgt. Golosini: Thank you for your search for our missing icon. As for Cajun State, in 1755, the British began a forced deportation of the French colonists of Acadia in Canada (today the area is called Nova Scotia). Most went to Louisiana, many settling in the southwest area of the state which we call Acadiana or Cajun Country. Hence, when they established one of our state universities here in Abbeville, they called it Cajun State University. Hope this helps."

The chief steps in just as I send the email. He looks as if he hasn't slept. He pours himself a cup of coffee and stands leaning in the doorway. "Did I ever mention my position's not civil service, like yours."

"Actually, you have."

"The UP wasn't very happy with me yesterday. Not one bit." He took a hit of coffee. "I told you. Spare no expense." And he wanders off. UP—University President

Inspector-General A.B. Acheampong of the Ghana National Police Service, sent his heartfelt condolences, adding he doubted the stolen tree would turn up in his beloved country. Then he extends me a personal invitation (including free accommodations at the National Police Academy in Accra on the lovely coast of the Gulf of Guinea) to come and visit.

The final email I open comes from a yahoo email address. It's a picture of a post card featuring a Christmas tree on a beach and the logo, "Having a nice vacation. Wish you were here—from the Bahamas with Love." It's part of a mass mailing to everyone on the university police department. Cute. At least the frats are having fun.

After re-checking with Captain Jeanfreau at the Abbeville PD, and learning they haven't come up with anything on the Christmas decorations thefts, I go out on campus and check with my limited sources—students who have been victims and like talking with me since I helped them. One reminds me her mother still wants me over for some crawfish étouffée and a little andouille (no, andouille is a food—Cajun sausage made of spicy smoked pork).

I step into the chief's office with a print out of the Bahamian post card.

"The lead's slim," I tell him as I drop it on his desk. "But you said, spare no expense, so I'm thinking a long weekend on Paradise Island might prove fruitful."

He gives me an expressionless stare and pops another nicotine gum into his mouth.

I sit across from him and he slides a piece of paper my way. "Well, mister hot-shot detective, I have a better lead."

Printed on the paper in the chief's careful handwriting is—Sheriff Elmer Geozophats, Yalobusha County, Mississippi, and a phone number.

"Give him a call." The chief almost smiles.

"Well son," says Sheriff Geozophats, "Glad you called. I talked to this here fool FBI agent in your Lake Charles Office about your missing Christmas tree. He wasn't interested. But he passed me along to your Chief Boone. Say, is your chief completely demented or what?" The man sounds suspiciously like Gomer Pyle.

I take a sip from my fresh cup of coffee before answering with, "What makes you say that?"

"Well, I never seen someone so gal-darn worked up over a Christmas tree. I mean, I know it's worth a lil' money and embarrassin' that it got pilfered right off your campus, but I think he was foaming at the mouth."

"He does that occasionally. A hereditary affliction."

Geozophats laughs. "I don't know as much about heredity as y'all university fellas, but I never heard of foaming at the mouth as a hereditary trait."

My turn to ask a question. "Sheriff, how did you know about our missing tree?"

"It's on Google under recent crimes, hit the bizarre crimes section. Ever since I got this new computer, one 'a them new-fangled Macintoshes, I'm addicted to Google. Yahoo too. Anyway, we got a group down in Coffeeville, just south of where I'm sittin' here in Water Valley, both in Yalobusha County, well, they refer to themselves as arborist liberators. Ran across them two year ago at a demonstration up at Ole Miss. They seemed like peaceful hippies, long hair, long skirts, tie-dye shirts.

"Took me a while to figure them out 'cuz the Google dictionary lists *arbor* as an axle or spindle which something revolves around something. It also means a shady alcove with trees forming the sides and a roof. Who the hell liberates axles or spindles or shady alcoves? Hell, it wasn't until Arbor Day, last April when I put it all together. Know anything about Arbor Day?"

"Not really. Think I've heard of it though."

"It's what we call a semi-holiday here in the great state of Miss-sippi, like Pecan Day. Arbor Day is a national day when people are encouraged to plant and care for trees."

There has to be a point to this—hopefully.

"Well, son. We had some suspicious tree disappearings ourselves last Christmas and this Christmas some Christmas trees been snatched from public places, like from the front of Jubal Early School, ever hear of Jubal Early?"

"Not really."

"Confederate raider. Sumbitch almost captured Washington city in 1864, put Lincoln hisself under fire."

I'll have to look that one up.

"Well, son, getting to the point, I put snitches out all over Yalobusha County and found out that my little hippie group of *arborist liberators* call themselves the ATL. Thought that was some derivation of Atlanta, only I got a reliable source that checked in last night, barely escaped with her life. She tells me ATL means Arbor Terrorist League. They free captive trees and give them a proper burial in a landfill two miles north of Coffeeville.

I'm taking notes and shake my head. I have to slow down.

"Son, we're getting some warrants together for Judge Caruthers to sign. He signs anything I put in front of him, the old coot. Can you send me a good picture of your tree, in case I come across it?"

"When are you going to execute the warrant?"

"Tomorrow mornin'."

I pull a map of Mississippi from my desk drawer. "Where is Yalobusha County?"

"East of Tupelo and just south of Oxford. You know, Ole Miss is here."

Been to a couple LSU games at Ole Miss, pretty school. All I know about Tupelo is it's near Tennessee and Elvis was from there. I look at my watch and at the map and figure it'll take me over eight hours if I took one of our police cars. We take the next ten minutes setting up a meeting time and place, getting directions, exchanging cell phone numbers and synchronizing our watches. Synchronizing, just like in the old spy movies.

The chief is sleeping in his captain's chair. I gently nudge him, then nudge him harder.

"Marcus!"

His eyes blink open and I sit across from him and go over it all and no matter how I put it, it sounds like so much horse manure. I close my notepad and say, "I could be there in a couple hours if you get me a helicopter. Spare no expense, remember?"

He sits up and says, "Take the newest car and Shrek. He lost the damn thing." The chief slides a Shell gas card, an Exxon gas card and a MasterCard toward me. "Rent a truck and bring it back if you find it."

He turns around and opens the small safe behind his desk and brings out a cash box. He counts out eight fifty-dollar bills and says, "You're going to Miss-sippi. They may only take cash."

"Got any Confederate money?"

"What?"

It takes Sgt. Komarovsky, AKA: Shrek, a little over six hours to get us to the rendezvous point, Myrtle's Café in Scobey, just off I-55, a few miles east of Coffeeville, Yalobusha County, Miss-sippi. I notified the sheriff via cell phone when we were getting close. At six a.m. sharp, I follow our sergeant into the café. Komarovsky wears a black army fatigue shirt with "Police" in white across his chest, black army combat pants with black army combat boots, pouches on his belt carrying pepper spray, a taser, a stainless-steel ASP retractable nightstick, two handcuff cases, a dozen pockets stuffed with other assorted police paraphernalia, including three different knives, and his back-up sidearm, a nine-millimeter version of the forty-five caliber Glock he wears in a canvas holster on his right hip.

I wear my usual work clothes, tan Dockers, a white shirt, tie, light jacket to conceal my Smith & Wesson nine-millimeter in its carbon-fiber holster on my left hip, one extra magazine in a canvas pouch attached to my dress belt and my handcuffs tucked into the belt at the small of my back. I also have my Louisiana state boot badge (look it up, Louisiana looks like a boot) clipped to my belt just in front of my weapon.

The sign on the highway declared Scobey had a population of 234 and the sign outside Myrtle's Café says it's open 24-hours and ladies are welcome. There are no ladies inside the café, just a burly cook behind the counter, a heavy-set waiter, six Yalobusha County Sheriff's deputies in their khaki uniforms and Sheriff Elmer Geozophats, who gives me pause a moment because—isn't Orson Welles dead?

"Well, son, I hope y'aller hungry. I just ordered up a passel a grub."

Passel is a relative term. I'd figured on a couple pots of coffee, eggs, bacon and toast, but didn't count on a hill of grits, ham steaks, pork tongues, lima beans, roasted kidneys (from what animal, I have no idea), gizzards (those are from chickens), deep-fried liver fritters, T-bone steaks, potatoes in various genres (hash-browns, roly-polys, waffle fries, mashed potatoes, creamed potatoes, potato pie and your everyday French fries, called freedom-fries on the menu—and I don't even want to go there) and of course, hush puppies.

The sheriff is too large to squeeze into a booth, so he perched himself precariously on a stool at the counter. Don't recall the names of the deputies, except three were named Calhoun, and that's their first name. They told me the next county is Calhoun County.

"We're not goin' all the way to Coffeetown, 'zactly," says Sheriff Geozophats as I sample my eggs, sunny-side-up, which are very good. "They have a compound on the Yalobusha County side of Granada Lake, only a couple miles from here."

I'd never seen Komarovsky eat before and don't want to anytime soon. He would be better served with a shovel. I have to keep ducking, not from flying food, but to keep the muzzles from pointing at me as he and the deputies pass around their loaded weapons and toss around their knives, some opened. Komarovsky, like so many present-day patrol officers, shaves his head and takes for his hero the lunatic character played too well by Michael Chiklis on *The Shield* TV show (I liked him better in *The Comish*). On our way up to Scobey, I'd mentioned *The Shield* was supposed to be fiction, not a training film. Shrek replied, "Too bad."

I climb into Sheriff Geozophats's Jeep SUV with one of the Calhouns, buckle up, expecting a maniacal ride along backroads. We go through backroads all right, but the Sheriff keeps the speed down and carefully negotiates the hair-turns, everyone in line behind us.

"Only way to keep ma' boys from tearin' out the undercarriages is to get in front and go slow," he says. He smells like pecan pie. I'm not kidding.

The clay is red and the grass bright green as we negotiate the piney woods, early morning sunlight dapple on the ground and on Grenada Lake to our right. The sheriff slows and turns down another backroad while the other cars peel off behind us to come up on the compound from different angles. I'm glad to see Komarovsky right behind us as the canopy of trees melts away and the lake lies sprawled to our right.

The sheriff points to the left at a log cabin with a satellite dish outside and telephone and electric lines attached to the roof. The land falls away behind the cabin and we wait for the others to get into position. There are no cars or trucks parked anywhere around and the sheriff comments, "I don't like the looks 'a this."

"There's a piece of paper tacked to the front door," Komarovsky says as he joins us outside the sheriff's vehicle. When everyone is in position we move in slowly. About twenty yards away, the sheriff calls out (man doesn't need a megaphone), "This here's the high sheriff. Y'all in the cabin. Come on out!"

Two beats later, he repeats the same order, then adds, "Y'all *don't* want us comin' in on 'ya!"

No response.

The sheriff waves to the nearest Calhoun and tells him to check what's tacked to the door. The deputy creeps over, both hands on his handgun. The sheriff and I are the only ones with our weapons holstered.

Calhoun looks at the paper tacked to the front door, nods, then opens the door and peeks in. He holsters his weapon and calls back, "The note's for you, Sheriff."

I follow the big guy up to the porch and watch Sheriff Geozophats snatch the note off the door. He instructs his men to search inside the cabin, "But don't make a mess."

He shows me the note, which reads: "Uncle Elmer. Sorry we had to leave early. We'll be back. Love, Dolly Simson."

"My niece," the sheriff says. "Got about forty of 'em. She was my *source* on this." He shakes his head. "Didn't think she'd play me like this, however."

Komarovsky comes rushing from around the cabin and calls out, "I found our tree!"

Behind the cabin, where the hilly land falls away toward the lake, a steep ravine lies half-filled with Christmas trees. Komarvosky shakes his head. "Ours has gotta be in there. It'll take some digging."

I made an immediate executive decision.

"Don't dig. Just get us some of those lights and ornaments, some of the good stuff. And see if you can find a white angel."

I turn back to the sheriff, "Do you happen to know where we could buy a twenty-foot spruce tree, this close to Christmas?"

"I just might."

"And where we can rent a truck to tow it back to Louisiana?"

"I just might."

I pull out the cash. "U.S. Grant's not usually popular around here," I say. "Except this particular portrait."

Komarovsky and the Calhouns secure us some of the better ornaments and strings of light and a large white angel to top off the tree while the sheriff and I examine the small manifesto found inside the cabin. It is simply put:

Arbor Terrorist League

We solemnly swear to liberate trees murdered by humans to be used in any ceremony and return said trees to nature. We will harm no human or animal in the process, however, we will not be deterred.

There are six signatures, including Dolly Simson, some of the signatures fancy, some scrawled, like the Declaration of Independence.

Sheriff Geozophats is true to his word, locating an eighteen-foot spruce for us (hope no one measures) and a one-way rental truck to haul it. I have Komarovsky drive the truck, since it has a regulator and we'll stay under the speed limit. Takes us ten hours to get back.

Chief Marcus Boone has called out the troops, as well as the guys from the physical plant, who would reinstall the tree, and a kid with a camera (probably from the university newspaper). All are waiting behind our police station, the chief in a crisply-starched uniform and smiling broadly.

"You gotta hurry," he tells me.

"For what?"

"Gotta get cleaned up."

"For what?"

"Got a meeting with the UP and VPHD. You're their new hero."

FRUIT ON THE BOTTOM

Maura Yzmore

I couldn't believe it happened again. Was I losing my mind?

I closed the fridge, took a deep breath, and called Ray at work.

"Did you eat my yogurt last night?" I asked.

"You know I don't touch that stuff. Why?"

"It's gone."

"What do you mean it's gone? Didn't you just buy a couple of four-packs, like, yesterday?"

"So, I'm not crazy," I said. "You saw them too?"

"Yeah, when I went to grab a beer. Figured you must be having your stomach issues again."

"Well, the yogurt's all gone now," I said.

"Weird," Ray said. "Are you sure you weren't sleep-eating? You've been getting kinda chunky lately."

I felt a spasm in my abdomen.

"No, I wasn't sleep-eating." I almost added he would've known that if he had stayed over instead of sneaking out after I'd fallen asleep, but thankfully I stopped myself. The last thing I needed was him berating me again for my clinginess, so I said I'd see him later and hung up.

I'd never had any sleepwalking experiences, but part of me wondered if Ray was right. If I had been getting up and eating in secret.

I turned the whole kitchen upside down, looking for empty yogurt containers, but found nothing.

Another painful twist in my gut.

I had to find out what was happening.

I had to get a camera.

The guy at the tech store was red-haired and freckled, with a warm, broad smile. His name tag said Ted. My shoulders relaxed as he walked me through the options, slowly and clearly and without condescension.

"So, what do you need the camera for?" Ted asked.

"To be honest, I need to figure out who's eating my yogurt."

"Yogurt?"

"Yeah. It's been disappearing from the fridge."

He smiled. "Is it the good kind, with fruit on the bottom?"

"Obviously."

"Then I say, whoever's eating your yogurt is a person of great taste."

I paused. "You don't think I'm nuts, do you?"

He chuckled. "Not at all. The yogurt's obviously missing and you don't know why. I admit I'm intrigued too."

"My boyfriend says I'm getting up and sleep-eating it." As soon as the words left my lips, I regretted it.

"So, what if you are? That's nothing to be ashamed of."

"I suppose you're right." My cheeks flushed with embarrassment. "Anyway, I think I want this one," I said and pointed to one of the cameras.

"Good choice." He smiled and proceeded to ring up the purchase. "I hope you solve your yogurt mystery. And then come back to tell me all about it."

I placed the camera in a top corner of my kitchen, above the window. It wasn't hard to install, or to set up to record directly to the cloud.

"Wow, look who got all techy," Ray teased as he inspected my work. "Are you sure it's gonna record anything?"

"Yes, I am." My abdomen painfully tightened. "Why do you have to be like that?"

"Like what? I'm just joking. You take everything so seriously." He opened the fridge to grab a beer, his thick neck and shoulders bent in a familiar arc. "I'll be in the living room, watching the game. I've ordered us some pizza. Oh, and I can't stay over. I have an early day tomorrow."

My gut felt like I was being stabbed from within. I leaned over the sink and took several deep breaths.

While I waited for the pain to subside, I remembered the two four-packs of yogurt I'd just bought. I grabbed a cup from the fridge, rolled back the silvery lid and quickly stirred, then shoveled the sweet cream into my mouth.

As bits of strawberry touched my tongue, I remembered the tech-store guy and smiled.

The next morning, the yogurt was gone. There was no trace of it, except for the one container in the trash that I remembered emptying myself.

I logged into the online account; the recording was right where it was supposed to be. I almost expected that Ray would be correct, that I was too clueless to get the camera to work.

The fridge, sink, and stove were on the left side of the screen. At the center was the island with two barstools. In the top right corner, I could see partly through the kitchen door.

I was really hoping for a ghost. A friendly ghost with a fondness for dairy.

Instead, around two-thirty, I saw Ray's feet as he walked out of my bedroom and past the kitchen, on his way out of the apartment.

Not long thereafter, the camera caught a faint shadow on the floor. Someone was moving along the wall to the far right, toward the windows. Whoever it was made sure to stay out of view, but it was a clear night with plenty of moonlight, and the camera was sensitive.

The intruder then darted in front of the windows, right to left, toward the camera. They grabbed and shook the device until the contact broke and the recording ended.

They were swift, very swift, but I needed no more than a split second to be sure.

I'd recognize the outline of that neck and shoulders anywhere.

"You're back!" Ted smiled. "Did you find your yogurt thief?"

"Sadly, yes."

"Oh." He seemed worried. "You OK?"

"Yes. Better than I've been in a long time, actually." Since I'd broken up with Ray, my stomach troubles had stopped.

"That's good to hear," Ted said. "Camera working OK?"

"The camera's great. Well, it's broken, but that's a long story."

"I could help you fix it."

"No need," I replied. "Actually, I am here because I need someone to help me eat a lot of yogurt."

"The good kind, with fruit on the bottom?" said Ted, with a warm smile.

FAIR IS FAIR

Brandon Barrows

I flopped onto my side, rolled back the other way, then kicked off the sheets, swung my legs to the edge of the bed, and sat up. I looked at the clock on the nightstand: two-fourteen in the morning. I was exhausted, but it was no good; I'd never get to sleep at this point. I wished I had a cigarette or a bottle, something to calm the yips, but I quit smoking in my twenties and I killed the last bottle hours ago. It hadn't helped and neither would lying here tossing and turning.

I switched on the lamp and dressed in the clothes I threw on the floor before I got into bed. I pulled my leather jacket from the closet, then moved to the dresser and plucked the motorcycle keys from the hook they spent ninety-percent of their time on. I was normally a summer weekend rider, but the weather was nice enough for early spring and I thought maybe some wind and some speed would clear my head. Anything that might let me forget the four-thousand-dollar mess I was in was worth a shot.

Ordinarily, four grand up or down wouldn't be enough to panic me. More than once, I'd lost two or three times that on bad sports bets. I always won it back before long. The problem was that the money wasn't mine to lose, and Colby Trading Partners, where I was an analyst, was about to undergo an outside audit. In the past, when I "borrowed" from my employers, it was simple enough to juggle things around until I was able to pay the money back. It was never more than a week or so, and the company was small enough that we all wore a lot of hats. My fiddling around with numbers that didn't directly involve my primary work wasn't anything unusual.

But this time, I didn't have a week. I didn't even have a day, and I didn't need to look at my watch to count down the hours. The auditors were scheduled to arrive at eleven that very morning. If one of the junior partners hadn't accidentally let it slip the day before, I would have been blissfully unaware right up until the moment the handcuffs were slapped around my wrists.

But forewarned isn't always forearmed. Not when you're out of time, out of cash, and out of options.

Now, I rode along the lake road, trying to enjoy the breeze, but failing miserably.

The Scout Bobber underneath me was a hell of a machine, but I was too much inside my own head to appreciate its power and speed. I was so preoccupied, in fact, that I almost didn't notice the flash of light winking through the trees ahead of me. When it came again, I eased off the throttle and gentled the brake, slowing until I reached the turn onto a secondary road that would take me closer to where I thought I saw the light. Sixty feet down that road, I cut the engine, rolled to a stop, and stared into the dark cluster of trees and brush that separated this road from the main one.

When nothing happened after a few seconds, I was ready to chalk it up to my imagination. Then the light came again and this time, I knew for certain that it was real. This wasn't the distraction I was looking for, but I was glad for it all the same.

I pulled the bike to the side of the road, shucked my helmet, and dug a flashlight out of the saddlebag. I didn't turn it on, though, not wanting to alert whoever was out there. Visibility wasn't good; the moon was only a sliver and the second I stepped off the road, it was like being swallowed up by the earth itself. All I could do was keep heading in the direction of the light and hope I saw it again.

Before long, my feet found what felt like ruts in the dirt. I cupped my hand over the end of the flashlight and risked turning it on, just for a second. In the brief glow, I saw the remains of a path, something vehicles once passed over frequently before the woods began to reclaim it. Before my eyes readjusted to the darkness, I saw the light again, much closer. I realized, too, that I could hear something now: the grunt of a man's exertion, coupled with a faintly metallic rasp.

I pushed forward as quietly as possible. Abruptly, the brush opened into a clearing. On the far side there was another, wider path that must have been part of the one I found. Sitting at the end of that path was an SUV, its white paint reflecting what moonlight there was, making it seem to glow. Perched on its bumper was a flashlight; its beam outlined the figure of a man, digging in the tough, still half-frozen soil. Next to him, lying on the ground, was what looked like a rolled-up carpet. The man's body breaking the beam of the light as he worked caused the flashes I saw.

I switched on my own flashlight and turned it on the other man. He dropped his shovel and threw up his hands with a gasp of surprise. I only saw his face for an instant, but I recognized him: Jonathan Thayer, one of the richest men in the state, if not this part of the country. He was a friend and occasional business partner of my boss.

"What? Who—?" Thayer sputtered. Sweat sheened his high forehead, a tie hung loose around his neck, his sleeves were rolled up, and there were dirt stains all over his white shirt. He didn't look much like a self-made millionaire just then. He looked desperate.

"Put out that damned light!" he shouted, finally recovering some of the command he was used to.

I moved the light, but I didn't turn it off. My brain churned uselessly for hours, trying to find a solution to my problem, and here it was. Whatever Thayer was up to couldn't be anything he wanted the world to know about. Nobody digs a hole at three in the morning for any reason that was legal. A man as wealthy as Jonathan Thayer should be more than happy to offer a modest fee for some assistance and some silence.

"Need any help, Mr. Thayer?" I didn't bother keeping the smile off my face or out of my voice.

A jolt went through Thayer just as if he licked an electrical outlet. He went stiff as a board, all except for his mouth, which flapped like a fish out of water. After a moment, he stumbled back to his truck, grabbed the flashlight from the bumper, and pointed it at me. "I recognize you," he said at last. "You work for Justin Colby."

"I sure do."

"What was your name again?"

"Does it matter?" My hand was shielding my eyes, but I let him see my smile. "I think what *you're* doing is a lot more interesting than anything I could say."

"I ..." he began. "I can explain this. I'm sure it looks—"

"Bad?" I finished for him, stepping around the hole and away from his light. I poked the rolled carpet with my toe. "Yes, it does."

"It's not what you think," Thayer protested.

"It's not what *I* think that matters." I squatted, careful not to turn my back to Thayer. I unrolled the carpet and saw what I both expected and feared: the pale, contorted features of a young woman. In the uncertain light, her skin was pearly, making the dark bruises on her throat stand out even more. I rolled the carpet back over her and stood.

"She's dead," Thayer told me, unnecessarily. "I did it, yes, but it was an accident."

I pointed my flashlight at the ground by Thayer's feet and studied the older man. Lit from beneath, his features took on something sinister, but I doubted he was dangerous. He didn't even look frantic anymore. He looked old and tired and drained, as if the game was over and he damned well knew it.

"I suppose you'll call the police now," he said.

"Not necessarily."

He stared quizzically at me, head slightly cocked. That wasn't the answer he expected.

"You want to tell me about it?" I asked.

Thayer bit his lip, and scrunched up his forehead in thought. It was a kid's gesture; plainly, I caught him off-balance. It took him a moment, but he made his decision.

"She was ... my mistress. She worked for one of my companies, just a junior sales executive. There was no reason I should have ever become aware of her, but we met by chance at a corporate event and after that, I couldn't stop thinking about her."

He turned from me to look out into the darkened woods. "Twenty-eight years with my wife and I never once cheated on her before Stephanie." He shook his head, as if he couldn't believe himself. "I don't know what it was about Stephanie that ... captivated me so much."

I could guess. Even in death, even with the terror of her final moments etched into her features, it was obvious that the girl had been very pretty.

"And?" I prompted.

He cleared his throat, licked dry lips. "We saw each other secretly for a few months. Tonight, she told me she was pregnant." His shoulders sagged. He backed up a few steps and sank down onto the bumper of his truck. "I offered to pay for an abortion, but she refused. I said I'd transfer her to another one of my companies, somewhere far from here, and make sure she was taken care of. She didn't like that idea, either." Thayer looked up at me. "She wanted to marry me. I told her it was impossible. We fought, it got very heated. She slapped me. I slapped her back, and then ..." He gestured vaguely towards the rolled-up carpet.

"I barely even remember it," he went on. He put his hands to his face, heedless of the dirt. "I was such a fool. Whatever there was between us wasn't worth risking everything for, and now I'm ... I'm a mur—"

"Stop," I cut in. "You don't need to say it. I get it. I understand."

Thayer raised his head. "You ... do?"

"Do you have another shovel?" I asked. "It won't be too long before the sun starts coming up, but between the two of us we can be done here in half an hour or so."

Thayer stared at me long and hard—so long, that I was beginning to think he'd never move or say anything again. Then he stood, opened the rear of his SUV, and produced a folding camp shovel. He handed it to me without a word. We got to work.

Soon, the carpet was buried—I refused to think of it as a body or about what I was helping Thayer do—and brush and detritus was scattered around in a way that looked natural. I examined the area from every angle and decided that it looked as good as we could manage. Unless someone knew where to dig, it would be a long, long time before anyone discovered this place—if they ever did.

Thayer stowed the tools in the back of his truck, then turned to me. Sweat poured off of his brow, he was smudged everywhere with dirt and there was a fresh tear by the armpit of his shirt. Before I started digging, I took off my riding jacket, but I was soaked, too, and I doubted I looked much better than Thayer.

"What now?" he asked.

I wiped my sweaty face with the tail of my shirt. "Now, I think I'd like a drink. You're buying, of course. I have my own transportation, so I'll meet you at the main road and follow behind, okay?"

Thayer sighed. "I suppose." He climbed into the SUV and, without turning on the lights, trundled slowly down the half-hidden path out of the woods.

I made my way back to the bike, trying to push the slimy feeling to the back of my mind, trying to let my elation at the solution to my own problem crowd it out. I never considered myself a criminal, despite what other people might think about my actions, but tonight I crossed a line. Not quite the line Jonathan Thayer crossed, but the law wouldn't see it that way, I guessed. What other choice was there though? There's one thing every gambler learns early on: when lady luck smiles on you, you don't question her.

Thayer's house was on the other side of the lake. The house itself nestled among ancient, well-groomed trees that clustered around it like protective parents, while a long, manicured lawn led down to a private strip of beach. There were no lights on when we pulled up to the front gate, but Thayer cut the headlights of his truck, so I did the same with the bike.

Thayer led me into the house through a side-door, dragging his feet like he was headed to his own funeral, listlessly flicking light-switches as he passed them. Whatever it was that once made him a captain of industry, a conqueror of the business world, it all leached out of him somewhere along the line.

Back in the woods, he seemed almost relieved to tell someone about what happened, and maybe even grateful for my help. The drive home, though, took about fifteen minutes and he clearly spent that time thinking. I had my own share of heavy thoughts on the ride over. We must have come to the same conclusion. Jonathan Thayer didn't know about my worries, and he didn't need to. The only thing he needed to know was how much this was going to cost him.

All I really needed was four thousand dollars and a couple of hours to square myself with Colby Trading. I wasn't worried about juggling the numbers or making the records look right. I'd handled that often enough. I just needed some cash and a chance to beat the auditors to the books. Four thousand was such a measly little number, though, and Thayer was so wealthy. Even if I didn't already know that about him, the house practically screamed money. And no matter my reasons, I *did* help him tonight, didn't I? My time and trouble had to be worth something.

"My wife is in New York for the week, taking our daughters on their annual shopping trip," he said, breaking the silence, "so we won't be disturbing anyone." I guess that explained Stephanie being so close to his home.

He stopped in front of an oak-paneled door and stepped inside. I followed and found myself in a study, its walls lined with leather-bound books. Three comfortable-looking chairs nestled in the center, facing each other in a triangle arrangement. Thayer moved to a portable bar in the corner, took two glasses from it and splashed bourbon into both. He walked back to me, thrust one of the glasses out, and when I took it, flopped into the nearest chair.

I sat in the chair across from Thayer, waiting for him to make the first move. I didn't have to wait long.

"How much?" he asked.

I sipped the whisky. It was better than any I ever tasted and only partially because it must have been very expensive. Despite everything, I let myself savor the moment. Having a little power was a fresh experience. I felt a smile tugging at the corners of my lips.

"Damn it, spit it out!" Thayer shouted, slamming his fist against the thickly-padded arm of his chair. He surprised me enough that I startled and slopped a little of my drink over the edge of the glass.

Thayer sucked in a deep, shuddering breath and let it out in a sigh. "I'm not a fool. I know what I am and I know that no one involves themselves in a murder without expecting something in return, so that tells me what *you* are. You're an opportunist who's found a gold mine. So just tell me how much already."

"Mr. Thayer," I began. I actually felt bad when he put it like that. The last hour or so gave me time to get used to the idea of being his accomplice, but he was making it sound pretty awful.

"I don't want to hear it." He drained his glass in one gulp, closed his eyes, and tilted his head back against the chair. "Just tell me how much money you want."

Whatever enjoyment I felt was gone. Jonathan Thayer looked very old and very tired and everything that happened—everything both of us did to bring ourselves to this moment—seemed small and tawdry. That didn't mean I was just going to walk out of there empty-handed though. I still needed to fix my own problem.

"Ten-thousand dollars," I said. It was a nice, round number that would let me pay back Colby and still feather my nest for a little while.

Thayer opened his eyes, glanced down at his glass as if hoping to see that it had refilled itself, then looked at me. There was no expression on his face, none at all. He reminded me of an uncle of mine who died peacefully in his sleep. Everyone at the funeral agreed he looked like he was truly at rest for the first time. I knew that wasn't what Thayer was feeling though. "And how much after that, Mister? ..."

"Don't go fishing, please," I told him. "And believe it or not, there won't be a next time. I know what you're thinking, but this isn't extortion."

"Then what is it?"

"We both have problems, Mr. Thayer. We're just helping each other out. I did do half the shoveling, after all, and fair is fair."

The older man barked a single humorless laugh, then slapped his hand down on his thigh and stood. He moved to the bar, set his glass on it, and took a painting of an old-timey fox-hunt off of the wall, revealing a barrel-style safe. As he moved the dial, he said, "Your name will come to me, sooner or later."

"But you won't do anything even if it does," I replied.

"No." He opened the safe and drew out a thick manila envelope. "I suppose I won't." He counted out a sheaf of bills, replaced the envelope, slammed the safe shut, and then stalked back to where I sat watching him. He held the money out to me. "Count it, if you like."

I took the bills. "I trust you, and you can trust me. I promise you that."

Thayer snorted. "You'll pardon me if I'm skeptical."

A response didn't seem necessary.

Under Thayer's weary gaze, I finished the rest of my drink, stood, and stuffed the cash into the inside pocket of my jacket. "I'll see myself out. Good night."

There was a bleakness on Thayer's face that I'd never seen before anywhere. It sent an unpleasant tingle down my spine, but I pushed it aside. Both of us would have to learn to live with the memories of this night. That was all there was to it.

It was crowding five when I got home. I would have loved some sleep, but that wasn't happening. I settled for a shower, clean clothes, and a little later, a McDonald's breakfast with the largest coffee they served. I was in the office at seven sharp and still wasn't the first one in. Traders are early risers by nature and even if the markets didn't open for more than two hours, there was plenty to keep them occupied. That suited me just fine.

It took some concentration and ingenuity, but by nine o'clock, the accounts were balanced and the records scrubbed squeaky clean. There was no way that anyone, no matter how deeply they dug, would ever be able to prove I'd taken a dime. A good accountant might suspect, but every cent was exactly where it was supposed to be, so there was nothing to even make an accusation about. I was in the clear and with the extra money I got from Thayer, hopefully I wouldn't have to dip into my employers' piggy-bank ever again.

I really meant it this time too. The last twenty-some-odd hours scared me straight and I intended to keep it that way. I actually felt good, I realized, like a massive weight was lifted from my shoulders. I glanced at my watch and decided there was plenty of time for a coffee break before the markets opened.

I was in the Dunkin' Donuts a couple of blocks from my office, sipping a twenty-ounce caramel latte and scrolling through local news on my phone when my relief melted clean away. The headline was simple, but eye-grabbing. LOCAL MAGNATE FOUND DEAD. The details were scant, but telling: when Thayer didn't make his customary seven-thirty appearance at his office, and his personal assistant couldn't reach him by phone, she drove out to his home to check on him, and found him dead of a self-inflicted gunshot.

I put my cup down. The sweet drink suddenly tasted like bile. I should have seen this coming. The strain on Thayer, the combination of his actions and my own, the look of utter hopelessness I saw on his face, it all added up in a way that should have been predictable. After I left, everything must have come crashing down on him and he decided he simply wanted nothing else to do with this world.

It shook me pretty badly. Not just that I probably contributed to a man's death, but the thought of what he may have left behind. If there was a note or anything like that, he might have explained himself, and if he remembered my name and mentioned my part in it …

But there was nothing I could do. I couldn't very well call the police and ask if Jonathan Thayer left a note and if so, was I mentioned in it by any chance? Even if the man didn't remember my name, he remembered who I worked for and that would be enough to eventually track me down. My underarms were damp and my palms felt cold.

I threw out the rest of my drink and walked back to the office on shaky legs.

I spent the remainder of the day stewing in my own cocktail of sweat and fear and I wasn't hiding it very well. I spent more time checking the news feeds on my phone than getting any work done. If I made it through the day, I'd pay for that later, but it was a problem for future me.

The auditors came and, a few hours later, went on their way without a word about anything amiss. Afterwards, Mr. Colby held an all-hands meeting to give us the good news. In the hallway, he stopped me, asked if I was feeling all right. I told him I was fine, but he sent me home, anyway, saying three-forty-four was as good a time to knock off as any. I was grateful for his kindness, but it made me feel even guiltier, since he was one of the people I wronged.

At home, I ran to my laptop without even taking off my shoes first. I spent over an hour scanning every news outlet I could find, but the articles on Thayer weren't updated with anything significant, just a few quotes from friends and business associates, and a plea for the family's privacy in this time of grief. There wasn't any indication that the police or anyone else suspected Thayer's suicide was anything but a depressed man taking a drastic solution. I began to breathe easier.

I relaxed in a long, hot shower, luxuriating in its warmth, imagining the stress and fear and guilt swirling down the drain and away forever. Now, nobody on Earth knew what Thayer did or about my part in it. I was really and truly free. I laughed out loud and wished I had something to toast myself with. I should have picked up a bottle on my way home, but I was so anxious the thought never crossed my mind. I decided I'd treat myself to a nice dinner out instead.

It was close to seven, and I was dressing to go out, when the doorbell rang. Ice surged through my guts, but I smiled at my foolishness and forced myself to relax. If the police knew anything, they would have found me long before now. I wasn't hiding.

In slacks, socks, and half-buttoned shirt, I went to the apartment door. A woman about my age, somewhere just north of thirty, stood in the hallway. She was medium height, average weight, brown hair, brown eyes, with a face that wasn't quite pretty, but you wouldn't call plain. She was dressed in a loose-fitting charcoal blazer and matching slacks. Her blouse was black. She could have walked out of any business office anywhere in North America. I'd never seen her before.

"Jason Brockman?" she asked by way of greeting.

"Yes, can I help you?"

The woman smiled. It made her more attractive. "Absolutely. My name is Deidra Tamlin. May I come in? You'll want to talk in private, trust me."

The ice in my belly splashed into my veins and spread all through my body. Warning klaxons were going off in my head, but I forced myself to play it cool. This woman wasn't a cop. She couldn't be. The cops wouldn't play it this casual. Until I knew who she was and what she wanted, there was no point in upsetting myself.

"Sure. C'mon in."

She entered the apartment. I closed the door behind her and gestured towards the living room. "I was just getting ready to go out," I told her.

She turned, the smile still in place. "This won't take long. I work—*worked* for Jonathan Thayer."

I swallowed past a lump in my throat. My heart beat a little faster. "I read about that. Suicide is a terrible thing."

"I agree, but I won't miss him too much." She seated herself, perched on the edge of the sofa. "He was kind of a prick to work for. Really demanding, used to his own way. I feel bad for his wife though. She's a sweetheart. His girls too."

I stood in the living room doorway, too tense to even think of sitting. "I don't understand why you're telling me this, Miss Tamlin."

"I feel worse for myself, though, you know?" she went on, as if I hadn't said anything. "I put in almost thirteen years with Thayer, waiting for my chance, waiting for the promotion that never came. And now I'm out of a job." She snapped her fingers. "Just like that."

"Sorry to hear, but—"

"I was the one who found Jonathan. You know that, right? You read about it, you said." The articles I saw didn't mention any names but Thayer's, but I didn't doubt her. Not when she was here, sitting on my couch.

"You're probably hoping he didn't leave a note," she said. "But he did." She reached into her pocket and drew out a folded sheet of paper. "This is just a copy I made, and there are others—both hardcopy and digital—plus the original, scattered around. I covered my bases. Besides a confession, Jonathan was really *very* detailed about what happened last night. He finally remembered your name, right after you left. It's a good thing all around that it somehow got ... *misplaced*, isn't it?"

My temples were pounding and my heart was beating so fast I was afraid it might explode. I thought I was free, my problems solved, and then this woman walked into my life with the biggest problem I could imagine. As if I was outside of my own body, watching from a distance, I heard my voice say, "What do you want?"

Her smile turned into a satisfied smirk. "We'll talk about a payment schedule later. I think we'll be able to do business together for a long time, don't you? But for now, since I'm out of a job, let's start with what Jonathan gave you last night."

There was a rushing in my ears, my fingertips tingled, and I couldn't take a deep enough breath. It was years since I had a panic attack, but I was right on the verge of one. I knew now how Thayer must have felt this morning, sitting in his own study, confronted by someone with the power to tear his life apart. The guilt came roaring up from the depths stronger than anything I'd ever felt before except for the fear. The fear was everything now. I was exactly where Thayer thought I was going to put him, never mind that I really didn't intend to go back for more. Deidra Tamlin had no such intentions.

She stood and walked over to me. "That's reasonable, I think. I did work for him a lot more than you, after all." A knowing little smile came to her lips. "And fair is fair, right?"

THE CHRISTMAS CAPER

Sharon Hart Addy

"Perfect!" Bailey mumbled to himself. The empty parking space next to the side entrance of the downtown community center suited his needs. He eased his car into it.

Twisting to look in his back seat, he checked to make sure the doors weren't locked. He didn't want to mess around unlocking them if he had to stash the loot in a hurry.

Satisfied, he opened his door and swung one leg out. The sight of his thick thigh in a green leotard stopped him briefly, but the black pointed shoes that came with the outfit brought his lopsided grin and reminded him of the makeup on his face.

Bailey sat back to check it in the visor's mirror. White face paint accented the rosy circles on his cheeks. A fringe of red beard along his jaw and almost completed the disguise. He didn't expect to run into anyone he knew on this side of town, but, if he did, he was sure they'd never recognize him.

After stepping from the car, he scanned the parking lot. Although every space was full, no one was around. Reaching into the back seat, he grabbed the wad of black plastic garbage bags. He unbuckled the costume's wide, black belt and stuffed the bags under it to make a belly. He adjusted the bundle so he could retrieve a bag easily, then redid the belt to hold them in place. After slapping on the green felt hat with the jingle bell tip, he felt ready.

When he entered the building, he found himself in a storage area. Bags and boxes of toys cluttered the floor. A line of tables in the center of the room held piles of stuffed animals, dolls, action figures, and games. Obviously, this was where the donations were sorted.

Bailey tip-toed around the table to listen at the door to the main room. A babble of voices told him a big crowd gathered for this party with Santa. The sweet aroma of pancakes, syrup, and sausage said breakfast was still underway. Bailey's uneven grin spread across his face. Everybody was busy. He'd be able to fill his bags and move them out before anyone saw him.

He grinned again as he realized that it wouldn't matter if they did see him.

Because of his costume, he looked like he belonged there. Didn't Santa always have elves hanging around? Of course he did!

Bailey slid a bag from the stash under his tunic and set to work. He selected toys with good resale value—teddy bears, dolls, trucks, and cars. His bag was almost full when the door to the main hall swung open. Bailey stiffened.

A tiny woman in an elf outfit appeared, dragging a clear garbage bag full of crumpled napkins and paper plates. "Nice outfit," she said. "It looks familiar." She chuckled at her joke.

Bailey swallowed to control his panic. He reminded himself that he knew this would happen. All he had to do was pretend he should be there. He asked, "Do you want me to take that out?"

She pushed the bag at him. "Sure. Thanks."

Bailey grabbed her bag and his. This is terrific, he thought. She thinks my bag's full of garbage. The plan's working.

Outside, he threw the real garbage into the dumpster and hauled his bag to his car. As he dug for the keys to his trunk, a battered truck pulled into the lot.

Quickly, Bailey tossed his loot in the back seat. Planning ahead saved him again!

The truck stopped behind his car. The driver called to him. "I've got some toys for the kids. Can you take them in?"

"Sure," Bailey answered.

The woman handed him a sack, said, "Merry Christmas!" and drove off.

Bailey waited until the truck turned onto the street, then he opened his car's trunk and dropped her donations inside.

When he returned to the building, he had the sorting room to himself. He grabbed what he wanted and deposited the bag in his trunk. After that, volunteers buzzed in and out of the little room. When someone was with him, he pretended to separate donations. When he was alone, he returned to his personal project.

As he carried the third bag out to his car, he gloated over how much money he'd make reselling the stuff at discount prices. He had just opened the trunk and was wondering if he could fit this bag in with the other one when he heard someone yell, "Wait! I'll help you."

Bailey turned and discovered Santa jogging up to him. Santa's belly wobbled back and forth and up and down. The sight made Bailey's lopsided grin spread cross his face.

Santa reached into the trunk and lifted both of Bailey's bags. "I'll take these."

Bailey's grin faded as he closed the empty trunk. He'd have to slip the bags out again when Santa and his real helpers weren't around. That might be a problem. The back room was getting awfully busy, but, if he couldn't retrieve these bags, he still had the one in the back seat. Bailey glanced at it as he walked past the car.

Santa asked, "Does that go inside too?"

Bailey swallowed hard.

Santa took that as a yes, pulled the bag from the car and handed it to Bailey.

Bailey followed Santa inside and slumped into a folding chair. This was turning into the worst job he ever tried to pull off. If he didn't snag at least one bag of toys, he'd be out money. Renting the costume wasn't cheap. Aside from that, wearing it was embarrassing. At least none of his friends knew what he was up to. He'd never live it down if they saw him.

A burst of singing invaded the room as the door to the main hall swung open. A lady elf appeared. "Santa, we're ready for you."

"I'll be there in a minute," Santa answered. He walked over to Bailey and bent over to talk to him privately. "A lot of these kids need male role models, a guy to show them it's better to give than receive. Instead of helping back here, you should be up front with me. What do you say?"

Bailey's mouth moved but no sound came out. Things were going from bad to worse.

"Great," Santa said. He patted Bailey on the back like they were old chums. "Here's what we'll do. You stand next to me while I talk to the kids. That way you'll hear what they ask for. If we've got it, you find it and give it to me. We'll start by handing out the stuff we brought from your car. Okay, Bailey?"

Bailey felt the makeup on his forehead crinkle as his eyes popped open. How did this guy know who he was? Could he really be Santa?

Santa pulled his beard down. Without the full beard and generous mustache, Bailey recognized his parole officer, Matthew Lewings.

"I've got to congratulate you, Bailey," Lewings said. "The costume's terrific but I'd know you anywhere. Now wipe that surprised look off your face and paste on your goofy grin. You're going to make this a merry Christmas for a lot of needy kids whether you want to or not."

What could he do? He pasted on his goofy grin and followed Santa.

JUST ANOTHER SMALL TOWN DEATH

Joseph Goodrich

In 1970 Margaret Breen used to invite neighborhood kids into her living room after school. She'd lead them through a scripture lesson and a hymn or two, then serve ice-cold lemonade and oatmeal cookies hot from the oven.

I'd been one of those kids. I thought about Mrs. Breen and those long-ago days as I studied the groceries scattered on the kitchen floor and waited for the ambulance to take her body away.

They wouldn't let her do that now. It's a different era. But those were less suspicious times—you knew your neighbors, you trusted them, they trusted you, and there was nothing wrong with a little after-school Bible study. In those days we'd all believed in God.

Manderton, Minnesota was a good place to live back then. Some of us still like it here; some of us never left. I'd gone to Police Academy in Minneapolis, and at first I thought I'd stay in the city. But in the end I came home. The town had been good to me, and I wanted to give something back. I wanted to help keep it safe for families like the Breens.

The Breens had the house two doors down from us. Slim ran the town's grocery store. Mrs. Breen was what they used to call a homemaker. Their son Brent was my age. We'd been good friends for a couple of years and spent a lot of time in the Breen rumpus room, reading *Mad* and *Famous Monsters of Filmland* and playing Pong and watching television. We were crazy about the Ed Sullivan Show and Dean Martin's All-Star Comedy Roasts. We loved the Roasts most of all, with George Burns and Rich Little and Milton Berle and Dom DeLuise and Arte Johnson—all those guys. They still make me laugh.

Which is more than I could say about the situation at the Breens'.

Up till then you might say my job was on the quiet side. I spent my time dealing with speeding drivers, beer-inspired brawlers, penny-ante shoplifters; hair-raising, sometimes, but nothing too horrible or consequential. But a murder was something else—especially when the victim was someone I'd known since I was a boy. Margaret Breen had been very kind to me over the years, almost a second mother for a time, after the death of my own and before my father remarried, and her murder hit me hard. It seemed that some of the city's darkness had seeped into Manderton.

Big-time cops would have called it just another small town death.

To me it was more like a death in the family.

The way I figured it, Margaret had returned from a quick evening trip to the grocery store and interrupted a B & E. She'd called Brent, who was at the Road Runner Lounge downtown. He rushed home to find his mother lying dead on the kitchen floor with her skull bashed in.

Officer Swenson came in, stepping carefully around the canned peaches and sardine tins and the grey cardboard container of eggs leaking yolk onto the linoleum.

Mickey Swenson's a Swede with blond hair and blue eyes who's roughly the size of a rich man's refrigerator. To look at him you'd think he was about as sharp as a box of bowling balls. You'd be wrong.

"How's Brent doing?"

"Hangin' in there,' Mickey said.

"Got his statement?"

He held up a steno pad. "Right here."

I read through Brent's statement, then handed the pad back to Mickey. "What do you think?"

"Seems to check out." He thought for a moment. "Mostly."

"Something fishy?"

"Don't know. Maybe."

"Guess I should talk to him."

Mickey nodded. "Good idea."

I went into the living room. Nothing had changed since we'd sung "I Know That My Redeemer Lives" in this room back when Nixon was president.

Brent was scrunched up on the couch. Judging by the liquor fumes coming off him, he'd been hitting it hard at the Road Runner. He looked miserable, but then Brent had always looked miserable. It'd been a long time since we'd watched dancing bears and impressionists and plate-spinners on Ed Sullivan, and life hadn't been easy for him. He'd taken over the grocery store after his father died and run it into the ground. He'd opened a used car lot that had closed in record time. Now he was assistant manager of the town's hardware store. Six months before his mother's death he'd given up his apartment near the lake and moved back home to save money.

"I'm sorry," I said to him. "She was a good woman, your mother."

"She was. Yeah. Thank you, Charlie."

"I'm gonna find who did this. I'm gonna see they get what's comin' to 'em. You know that, right?"

"I know you'll get them. You always do."

"I'm gonna try, anyway." I gave him a pat on the shoulder. "You're pretty shook up right now, so I'm gonna leave you be. But I'll come back tomorrow and we'll talk some more then."

He looked up at me with his bleary eyes. "I told Mickey everything I know."

"You might think of something else later."

"Like what?"

"Well," I said, "what they might have took. You gotta check to see what might be missing."

"Nothing's missing."

"You sure about that?"

"I don't know. I guess."

"You gotta check on that, you see? In the morning I'll come over and—"

He hauled himself off the couch. Words poured out of him in a shaky stream. "I told Mickey everything, Charlie. I was at the Road Runner. With Shelley. We were in a booth at the back. My phone went off, but I let it go to voicemail. Then I thought, well, maybe I should check it—it might be Mom. It *was* Mom. She thought someone was in the house and I'd better get home quick. And I said ... I said I'll be right there, Mom. Don't worry. It's probably nothing. It's ..."

He blinked rapidly and swallowed hard to keep the tears back, then let his head sink onto his chest. The silence stretched and stretched.

I didn't know what to say, so I headed back to the kitchen.

After the body had been removed, Doctor Faul gave Brent a quick examination and a sedative. I took a final look around the room. 1970 seemed very close just then, as if Margaret might walk in at any moment.

But she wouldn't.

I meant to find out who was responsible for that.

The next morning we had breakfast at the Gobbler cafe. We'd been up late talking the night before, and Mickey came right back to the subject that had kept us up so late: Brent Breen.

"I'm not *saying* he did it," Mickey insisted. "Though I think he did. This break-in set up's 'bout as phony as it can be. I'm just saying you oughta consider it."

"I have."

"Look at the facts, Charlie. There's a lot of motive here."

"Such as?"

"He's damn near broke, for one. Everyone knows he owes a lot of money to a lot of people. Two: He wants to start a new business, but to do that, he—"

"He wants to start a new business?"

"You didn't know? He wants to buy the old Thompson Hotel and turn it into something. Boutiques or whatever. You know—little shops for stuff."

"Who told you this?"

"Dave Fiola."

"No-one would give him the money to buy the Thompson."

"Exactly. That's why he killed his mother. To get the money—"

"To buy the Thompson," I finished.

"Exactly. He inherits."

"Interesting," I said, and stirred some half-and-half into my coffee.

"Another thing." Mickey crossed his fork and knife on the plate and pushed it aside. "The house was torn up, but he says nothing's missing without even looking. And when he does check, I'll bet nothing *will* be missing. How do you explain that?"

"The killer panicked. He wasn't gonna stick around with a dead woman lying there on the floor."

"Okay. Maybe. Sure. But explain this to me. She comes home from the grocery—someone's in the house—she calls Brent. Why not the police? Why not us first?"

"He was her son."

"We fight crime for a living. He doesn't."

"I don't rule him out," I said. "I don't rule *anyone* out, as a matter of fact. But there's one thing you keep forgetting."

"And that is?"

"You've seen Brent's phone, right? You listened to the message? The call from his mother came in at 9:52 p.m. At 9:52 p.m. he was at the Road Runner lounge. He was there when the crime took place. If you can explain me to me how he could beat his mother's brains in at the same time he's three miles away at the Roadrunner with

Shelly Torgelson, I'll arrest the son-of-a-bitch now." I slid off the stool. "I think it's your turn to pay the bill."

We went through our paces. We interviewed the neighbors. We talked with Shelly Torgelson and the Road Runner's bartender and anyone who'd spent time with Brent on the night of his mother's death. Shelley backed up Brent's story. He didn't leave the bar from the time he arrived to the time he got his mother's call. Denny the bartender told us the same thing, with a slight difference: Brent had gone off to the men's room at one point.

"How long was he gone?" I asked.

"How long does it take?" Denny said. "He goes in, couple minutes later he comes out, sits back down with that good-looking blonde, checks his phone—and freaks out. He says his mother's being robbed and he bolts out of the place."

That left us just about where we'd come in. We did everything we could—I made sure of that—but the net result was still a big fat goose egg.

Brent was still our prime suspect.

Hell, he was our *only* suspect.

For all the good it did us.

There was a big turnout for Martha Breen's funeral. Brent was in terrible shape. He broke down at the graveside and had to be helped away. Whether his tears were from sorrow or from relief, I couldn't tell.

We all went back to what we were doing before Margaret was killed, never expecting that a big surprise was coming our way.

It wasn't the size of Margaret Breen's estate, which was more substantial than anyone had imagined. It wasn't the fact that Brent didn't sink his inheritance into the Thompson Hotel scheme. It wasn't the fact that he sold his mother's house, then his own, and put *that* money in the bank along with what he'd inherited. It wasn't even the announcement that he and Shelley Torgelson were going to get married.

Actually, that was a bit of a surprise. Shelley had been the best-looking girl in the class of '79 with her Dorothy Hamill wedge and Jordache jeans. Everyone agreed that Brent was a lucky man.

No—the big surprise was that Brent was leaving town. He was off to the big city, off to Minneapolis, where he and Shelley's cousin Steve were going into business together. Steve owned a candy manufacturing business and was looking to expand.

Money in the bank, the girl of his dreams, success in business ... Life for Brent

Breen, who'd previously been known as the sad-sack town joke, had finally become a thing of sweetness.

Mickey slapped a thick square of paper onto the desk. "Take a look at that, will ya?"

I picked up the creamy-white parchment invitation to Brent's farewell party. It was being held, of all places, at the Road Runner Lounge. 7:30, Friday night. Casual dress. Handwritten under this was: *Love to see you guys!—Brent.*

"Son-a-bitch," I said.

We got to the Road Runner about a quarter past eight.

Brent and Shelley Torgelson and company were crowded around a table near the back, hooting and hollering. Brent was the loosest and loudest of them all.

Mickey and I stayed by the bar. I wasn't sure what I was watching or waiting for, and neither was Mickey. An hour went by. Nothing got any clearer. It was just another evening. No mystery here—no solution, either.

Mickey tapped me on the arm. "Charlie?"

"Yeah?"

"You know where this is getting us?"

"Zipville."

"Exactly. Let's get out of here."

A burst of laughter came from Brent's table.

I turned to look, started to say something—and stopped. From the other side of the room, I heard the voice of Margaret Breen.

Shelley and the others were laughing wildly at Brent.

"Jesus loves us all," he was saying in a perfect imitation of his mother. "So we have to love everyone, too. Even those who hurt us. *Especially* those who hurt us. So what does the Lord want us to do?"

"Rotten little bastard," I said to Mickey.

Brent looked from one of his guests to another, his eyes glowing with malice. "Whoever gives me the right answer gets an extra oatmeal cookie. What does the Lord want us to do?"

"What?" his friends cried.

"Turn the other cheek!" Brent cried, then wagged his head frantically from side to side. Shelley and the others exploded with laughter. Brent cackled along with them.

"I'd like to see him behind bars," I said. "Not sitting in one."

"How'd he do it, Charlie? How'd he kill her? How could he be in two places at the same time?"

"Beats the hell out me," I said. "You can only *be* in one place at a time."

More laughter erupted at Brent's table, all at his mother's expense. I have to say it shocked me. I mean, we all go through those periods when our folks can't do anything right—they don't understand us, they're holding us back, all those teenage things. Eventually you grow up and get over it and move on with your life. But Brent was stuck; something in him had failed to thrive. I don't know whose fault it was or why it turned out that way, but it was obvious that Brent blamed his mother.

And hated her.

"I'd like to go over there," Mickey growled, "and ring his chimes. We've got his number and we can't do a damn thing about it."

His number ...

Two places at once ...

Something shifted in my mind.

The pieces of the puzzle snapped into place.

Mickey was right: Brent *couldn't* be in two places at once. But there was a way to make it seem as if he had.

I searched my pockets. I'd left my cell phone at home, re-charging. I stuck out my hand. "Give me your phone."

"Why?"

"Just give me your phone, dammit."

"Okay, okay, hold on." Mickey dug into the pocket of his jacket and brought out his cell phone. "Here you go. Jeeze."

"Go talk to Brent."

"Why?"

"Just do what I say. Go talk to him. I'm going to call him. And then be prepared for whatever happens."

"What's gonna happen?"

"I'm not exactly sure. But whatever it is, just be ready."

"You're the boss." Mickey went off to Brent's table.

I dialed Brent's cell.

"Hello," I heard him say.

"Hello, Peanut," I said, using his mother's pet name for him.

I was also using his mother's voice.

"How's your little party going, Peanut? Are you having fun?"

I watched him as he tried to break the connection, but Mickey enveloped Brent's wrist with one of his giant hands, and squeezed. The phone dropped out of Brent's grasp and into Mickey's. The table around him had gone silent. So had the rest of the bar. Mickey switched on the speaker phone. I took a deep breath and continued. I could hear my words coming out of the phone across the room, tiny and tinny in the distance.

"It's your mother. You killed me in the kitchen one night and made it look like a break-in. Remember? Then you took my phone with you to the Road Runner and called your *own* phone in the bathroom and left a message. You imitated me and said you were in danger. Then you rushed home, put my cell phone next to my corpse, and called the police. Your old pal Charlie Wright came over. He's at the bar right now."

Brent swiveled around, crazy-eyed. I gave him a neat wave of the hand.

"You left all kinds of holes in your story, Peanut. But they couldn't break your alibi, so you were safe. But you're not safe anymore. Charlie figured it out. He knows how you did it. Mickey Swenson knows too. And so does Shelley. And so does everyone at your table. And pretty soon every—"

Brent stuck it out longer than I'd expected. But in the end he broke. He kicked his chair aside and skittered toward the back door of the bar like a very frightened and very clumsy rabbit.

He didn't get far.

Brent never did, try as he might, and that was part of his problem.

I drove out to the cemetery to place flowers on Margaret Breen's grave. I thought about those days when she'd have us kids in for oatmeal cookies and gospel readings. She'd meant well. She tried to teach us something. She'd tried to instill in us principles that could help us through our lives ... and into heaven afterwards. I no longer believed in heaven, but that didn't change the way I felt about her. It didn't lessen my gratitude.

While I was there I paid my respects to my father and my mother and my grandparents. Though they were gone, they lived on in me—and so would Margaret Breen. I thought about her and all the years gone by so quickly. I knew where those years had gone—into living a life, or trying to—as surely as I knew they could never be regained.

Walking back to the car, I thought about Brent, too. Our friendship had faded with the passage of time. He'd become a stranger to me—and to himself. I remembered the days when we'd camp out in the Breens' rumpus room, watching old movies and working on our impressions of Jimmy Stewart and Humphrey Bogart and Peter Lorre. Brent's impressions were always much better than mine. He had a real knack for impressions, no doubt about it. But I wasn't too bad at 'em, either. Not too bad at all …

A HUNGARIAN CHRISTMAS

Vicki Weisfeld

Bert held out the distinctive aqua-colored box and offered a wobbly smile.

"What's this?" Veronika recognized Tiffany blue when she saw it and knew they couldn't afford it, shouldn't indulge themselves. For now, every penny should go toward their February 14 wedding or essentials for their new apartment. But curiosity about what was inside that box was building fast.

"It's Hungarian Christmas!" Bert exclaimed.

He was right. It was December 5, St. Nicholas's Eve, and St. Nicholas's Feast Day, December 6, was well-celebrated in Veronika's family. She'd told him about it in mouth-watering detail—the bright red fisherman's soup, the fragrant stuffed cabbage, the luscious poppy seed and walnut rolls, the sweets. In the press of everything, she'd almost forgotten.

"And," he continued, "you told me every Hungarian girl has to have a present on Hungarian Christmas."

She'd said that? "Right." She flushed.

Veronika untied the white satin ribbon, removed the box lid, and took out the small case within. Really, she couldn't resist. In for a penny, she thought. Slowly she lifted the case's hinged lid and gasped. "Oh! It's beautiful! But, Bert, did you just win the New Jersey lottery? Or what? How can we afford this?"

The ring had a brilliant yellow stone in the center—a citrine she supposed, or a kind of topaz. It was huge. Huger than huge. And surrounded by diamonds, each the size of a large peppercorn, though realistically, she knew they were probably cubic zirconia or manmade.

"Forget the lottery. You robbed a bank." She hadn't taken her eyes off the ring and could barely catch her breath.

"Nothing's too good for the future Mrs. Harkness. Not on Hungarian Christmas, when every Hungarian girl—" As he spoke, she rotated the box so he could admire the extravagant ring. He took a look. "Oh, my God!"

He collapsed into the chair opposite her in their tiny living room. "That's not—I didn't—I bought a pair of earrings." Small ones, in fact. Which seemed even smaller compared to the size of the ring. Not even gold. Sterling silver. His face reddened. Now he was mesmerized by the mysterious ring. "Not that I wouldn't buy you a ring like this if I—if we—but I didn't." He sounded miserable.

"We can't—"

"No, we can't."

Veronika sat back, confused. "So, you're saying you bought me a nice pair of earrings. Not this. So, how did you end up with it?"

"I don't know. I can't imagine."

"What was the store like when you were there?"

"Not too busy. I took a late lunch and went then. A nice older woman—probably about 40—waited on me. She was very patient. Price-range challenge and all ..." He screwed up his face, trying to remember. "Oh. There was a lively group of guys on the other side of the store, in the ring department, in fact. They were Asian—Korean or maybe Japanese, I think. They turned buying a ring into a group project. Lots of enthusiasm."

"That's it! The boxes got switched."

Bert pondered the possibility. "That seems unlikely. I don't see how it could have happened. I gave the woman my credit card and she came back with my receipt and the box in a little Tiffany's bag—I saved the bag for you—and for some reason, maybe the size of the purchase, the men were escorted into an office to pay. They insisted on paying cash, and the sales person seemed a little hesitant. But they must have worked it out, because the men did come out with a bag. I think."

"I'm calling Paul and Tommy. We need help here."

"Why? Why do we need your brothers?"

"Because," she said, picking up her phone, "something's very wrong about this."

"I can just take it back," he said, talking over her greeting to Paul. She turned to Bert, and told her brother to hold on. "And leave Tiffany's in handcuffs? A valuable ring like that doesn't just get switched. Who knows what they'll think really happened? Collusion between you and an employee? Whatever? But then you got cold feet and walked in with the evidence? No way. You need protection." She returned to the phone. "Paul, we need you, ASAP. And bring Tommy." She disconnected.

"But—"

"It isn't enough to be innocent, my darling. Others have to believe you're innocent. That's what saves you. And Paul, Tommy, and I *do* believe it." She gave him a hug. "Thank you for remembering Hungarian Christmas."

The brothers arrived within the half-hour, eager to help their little sister and uniquely qualified to do so. Paul was a Jersey City police detective and Tom a criminal attorney. If Veronika needed something, they were all in, personally and professionally.

She and Bert explained the puzzling situation, one piece of which was how to return the ring, safely. Tommy said, "You can't just get on the train tomorrow morning with it in your pocket. Something that valuable, somebody may be watching."

"Why were you in Tiffany's in the first place?" Paul asked.

"I was buying Veronika's Hungarian Christmas present, since that's when all Hungarian girls need a present."

The brothers glanced at each other, eyebrows raised. Tommy winked at Veronika. "Nice."

Because it was past closing time, they couldn't just call the store for advice on the safest way to return the ring. While Tommy and Bert debated the transport problem, Paul went out front to make calls.

Veronika defrosted several trays of stuffed cabbage in the microwave and cooked bow-tie noodles. The aroma of a traditional Hungarian dinner soon filled their little second-floor apartment. It had a tiny kitchen and no dining room, so with the four of them around the table, space was tight. When Veronika brought them their plates, heaped with steaming cabbage rolls, they couldn't help noticing the ring glittering on her right hand. "Holy *frijoles*, what a rock!" Paul said, picking up his phone to read a text.

A moment later, the doorbell rang. "Got it," he said, hurrying to the front door. He returned to the kitchen table with a beefy white guy he introduced as "J.T. Taylor, NYPD."

Veronika brought J.T. a plate, and they shifted around the table to make room. J.T. caught a look at Veronika's right hand and, wide-eyed, said, "That it?"

"Yes," they all replied.

"Wow! Just a guess, but I'm thinking Tiffany's will want that back."

"J.T. is our security squad," Paul said.

"You're gonna need it," J.T. said.

Veronika's eyebrows peaked in a question.

Paul said, "Why? Because I'm not driving into Manhattan with a gigantic piece of stolen jewelry worth tens of thousands of dollars."

"It's not stolen," Bert objected. "It was a mistake."

"Where'd you get this guy?" Tommy asked her, patting Bert on the back. Then, to Bert, "Did you pay for it?"

"Well, no, but someone did."

"Right. And they'll say you stole it from them."

Bert frowned, as if trying to wrap his mind around such bizarre behavior. "I get that, I think, but ..."

Veronika was pushing her food around, not eating. "I don't understand it either. *Is* the ring stolen? The Asian guys paid for it. It doesn't make any sense."

J.T. said, "Ten to one—*hundred* to one—they go back to Tiffany's in the morning, show their receipt for the ring and the box with the earrings Bert bought and demand their money back."

"So they'll claim there was a switch?"

"Could there have been?" Paul asked Bert.

"I don't know. Maybe, I guess. We all happened to leave at the same time, and there was a lot of jockeying at the door."

"Happened to?" Tommy's lawyerly skepticism was showing.

Flustered, Bert continued. "There was the usual 'After you,' 'No, after you' kind of slapstick. Since there were five or maybe six of them, one ended up squeezing through the door just as I did. But he was laughing, not looking suspicious or ... furtive. They were all in a happy uproar, and I didn't think anything of it."

"Classic brush pass and switch," J.T. said.

"Don't go all Spycraft on us," Veronika said, and J.T. shrugged. "Sorry, but I still don't get it. Even if Tiffany's will give them their money back tomorrow, right then and there, and not make them wait for the insurance or an investigation or whatever, they're no better off than they were."

"Unless, of course, they didn't really have that kind of money to begin with," said Tommy, whose clients had needed him to investigate his share of fraud and money laundering cases.

"What did they pay with then?" Bert asked.

"Someone else's cash. Or a check, drawn on a new and very temporary account," Tommy said.

"We can assume that if they paid by check, it wasn't going to bounce," Tommy said. "Or if they paid cash, it wasn't counterfeit."

"That's why the sales person took them into the office for the transaction, to make sure the money was solid," said J.T. "After Paul called me, I put out some feelers for similar crimes. We'll see if anything turns up."

"Exchanging dirty drug money for clean Tiffany money?" Tommy wasn't letting go of the money laundering angle. "Or the sales associate who checked them out was in on it?"

They pondered these possibilities until Veronika interrupted. "But see, they went in, spent a lot of money, and you say they'll go in again and get it back. How are they any better off?"

Paul fixed her with a sad stare. "I suppose I should be glad you don't get it. The only way this caper pays off is if they get the ring too. I thought you were my smart kid sister. I'm surprised it's taking you so long to figure it out."

"This makes me mad," she said, dropping her fork onto her plate and blowing past the threat Paul had just suggested. By the look on her brothers' faces, that was not the response they expected.

"Why, hon?" Bert asked.

"They're counting on us to be as dishonest as they are. That we won't call up Tiffany's immediately and tell them we have the stupid ring and are returning it pronto."

"You can bet they'll be there first thing in the morning to beat you to it, just in case," said J.T. "They'll have the ring by then too. They think."

"I wish I'd never gone in there," Bert muttered. "But it's Hungarian Christmas—"

"What?" J.T. asked.

"And every Hungarian girl—"

"Skip all that," Veronika interrupted. "But do you really think they'll try to get the ring back? How do they even know where we—"

At that moment, the lights went out.

"V, you and Bert go into the bedroom and stay down." Paul's tone didn't invite argument. They stumbled out of the kitchen guided by the flashlight in Bert's phone. Veronika glanced over her shoulder and saw Paul's face lit by his phone's screen, his big hands flying over the keypad.

She and Bert huddled on the floor by the bedroom closet. He gathered her into his arms and held her close, to stop her shivering. "I never imagined anything like this," she said. Her voice quavered, but she was dry-eyed.

"Me neither. It seemed like such a simple thing. A simple gift." He gave her a squeeze. "For my sweetie."

"I know. Not your fault. At all."

The bedroom overlooked the building's front lawn, and some kind of commotion was taking place out there, but the apartment itself remained eerily quiet until someone pounded on the front door.

"Police! Open up!"

Paul asked loudly for a code word and must have gotten it, because the door opened. Veronika scooted across the floor, patting the top of her vanity for her hand mirror. She duck-walked to the bedroom window and sat. J.T. stood in the bedroom doorway, his back to them, on guard. She slowly lifted the mirror, tilting it for a view out of the window and into the front yard below. In the pools of light cast by the streetlamps, she could see maybe fifteen men, most of them in uniform. The ones not in uniform were definitely Asian. "Wow!" she said.

"Clever you," Bert said. "What do you see?"

"Our rescue party. The Jersey City cops are hauling a bunch of Asian guys into cars." Sirens erupted on the street.

Out in the hallway, someone walked up to J.T. and spoke to him in a low voice she recognized as Tommy's. The lights came on.

"You can come out now," he told Veronika. He laughed when he saw her with the mirror. "You saw Paulie's guys take them away? You remembered that trick."

"You taught it to me," she said, "so we could spy on our sisters and their boyfriends."

Several of Paul's fellow Jersey City officers plus Paul and Tommy and J.T. were crammed into the standing-room-only living room. Paul introduced Bert and his sister. "Is that it?" each one asked, as she shook their hands and they got an eyeful of the gorgeous ring.

"I forgot I had it on. I'm getting so used to it." She reddened, embarrassed she'd put it on and kept it there. That didn't trouble them, though, and they spent time admiring it.

"Don't get *too* used to it," Bert said. "Because tomorrow ..."

"What do you think it's worth?" an officer asked.

Paul called over a colleague. "When you worked that jewelry store heist, did you get any idea what a ring like this would cost?"

"No, man. It all depends on the stones. These are big though."

Veronika looked at the ring thoughtfully. Citrine and man-made diamonds would be on the low end of the price-scale, then up from there. To her, the central stone had good color, was clear and nicely cut for sparkle, and its size stretched credulity. But what did she know?

"When we go into the city tomorrow, Bert, and Tommy, and I will ride in J.T.'s sedan." Paul instructed. "I'll want one of our SUVs riding in front of us and one in back. Lights and sirens until we reach the tunnel. I don't think there'll be any problem, but just in case. Are there more gang members out there? I dunno. When we get to the store, we'll escort Bert inside and stay with him. Even if they know we have the ring, they won't know which one of us has it."

"From the store's point of view, having J.T. and Paulie there is pretty good evidence that Bert's on the up-and-up," Tommy said. "You were right to think the store might hassle him. But they won't if we're there."

"One more thing," Paul told his colleagues. "Make sure your prisoners don't make any phone calls until we get this done. They might tip off someone that Bert—or Veronika—still has the ring. I've had enough excitement for one night."

The Jersey City officers left, but Paul and Tommy and J.T. stayed the night— the brothers on the pull-out sofa and J.T. in the recliner. When Veronika apologized about that, he said, "Believe me, I've slept worse places. At least it's dry."

Two Jersey City Interceptors pulled up in front of the apartment building at 9:30 the next morning. With J.T.'s unmarked vehicle between them, they'd make up a three-car convoy through the Holland Tunnel and into Manhattan. Estimating a half-hour trip, they expected to arrive at Tiffany's right when it opened. "I'll give them a heads-up from the car," Tommy said.

Bert put the ring box in his jacket pocket. "I haven't done anything wrong," he whispered to Veronika as he gave her a good-bye hug. "Why am I so nervous?"

"All these cops," she whispered back. "Paulie even makes *me* nervous sometimes."

As they drove away, J.T. shot a glance into the rearview and saw Bert hunched in the back seat next to Tommy. He'd seen plenty of anxious passengers before and kept the conversation light—holiday plans kind of thing.

Bert spoke up unexpectedly from the back seat. "The lights in the apartment. What happened with the lights?"

"That was us," said Paul. "Our guys were in position on your block, and when the gang arrived, they signaled their man in the basement. He doused the electricity for your apartment so the would-be intruders couldn't see inside. After the gang was safely in custody, they called him again, and he flipped the electricity back on. Just a little diversion. To make you and V safer. Create confusion."

"Oh." Bert said. "Thanks."

J.T. and Paul silently signaled each other as they approached the tunnel. They and the officers in their escort had agreed it was the likeliest danger point, as traffic slowed to enter. The three cars pulled in tight. If Bert had been watching, he would have seen the detectives' shoulders visibly relax once they exited the tunnel rotary onto Manhattan's Sixth Avenue.

Tiffany's was expecting them. The manager met them just inside the door, introducing himself as Connor Williams. He walked them to an elevator, they took it up a couple of floors, and he guided them down a long hallway to a small conference room. Waiting for them there was the store's public relations director, a man named Long.

Paul described what they believe happened the previous afternoon. While Williams called up the security cam footage, Bert said, "I just wanted to get my fiancée a nice present for Hungarian Christmas."

"For what?" PR Director Long asked.

"Hungarian Christmas. December 6."

"That's today," Long said. Bert nodded.

"Let's just see what we have here." Williams was keying in codes and time parameters on a laptop, and fast-forwarded to the relevant section.

"Those men made quite a stir in the store, and now that you point it out, their behavior could have been a deliberate distraction. Our staff got tired of them, frankly, so stopped paying close attention."

"Bunch of goofballs," Long said in a very un-Tiffany, un-PR-like way.

The manager turned the screen, enabling his visitors to see the footage. The confusion at the exit was clear and the exchange of bags seamless. Bert was jostled at just the right moment so that he was unlikely to notice the release and reapplication of pressure on his fingers when the man behind him took his bag and replaced it with another.

"Those are the guys all right," Paul said, adding for Williams's benefit, "We arrested all six of them last night outside Mr. Harkness's apartment."

The manager's phone buzzed. "I'll take this." He listened a moment, then said to the group, "A hysterical Asian woman is here, claiming we mixed up her husband's purchase. She's waving the receipt around and has a box with some inexpensive silver earrings."

Bert winced, and Williams saw it. "Very pretty, but not in the same price range as the ring, of course. Should they show her up here?" he asked.

"Sure, why not?" J.T. said. "Taking a meeting with two law enforcement officers might give her a jolt."

The agitated woman was brought to the conference room. The men all had coffee, but she wasn't offered anything. Clearly, she'd been taught that the best defense is a good offense and had no intention to be anything other than totally unreasonable. Every other sentence included the words "money back, money back!" In the midst of this commotion, J.T. was quietly reading his texts.

"I'd like to introduce you," Williams said, "and you are?"

"Money back!" she practically screamed. In the confined space, her shrill voice reverberated.

He tried again to introduce them, but she wouldn't listen. Williams shrugged and gave it up. He tapped the keyboard. When she took a breath, he turned the laptop toward her. "You say your husband bought this ring." He glanced at the description on the receipt she'd produced.

"Bought. Didn't get."

Before she could start demanding money again, he pointed to the laptop screen and asked, "Is your husband in this picture?" It showed the cluster of Asian men shortly before the scrimmage at the store exit.

"He right there!" she shouted, pointing.

"And who are those other men? Can you identify them?" Tommy asked in a calm tone.

"His brother and cousins and friends. They help him pick expensive ring. But no get!"

"True, he didn't get it," Williams said. "And here's why." He advanced the video to the point where the exchange was made. "Your husband's accomplice exchanged bags with Mr. Harkness." He gestured to Bert, sitting across the table.

Bert's presence seemed to surprise her, but she recovered quickly. Spluttering, she prepared to launch into another tirade. J.T. asked in as nonconfrontational a tone as he was probably capable of, "If it was your husband who bought the ring, why isn't he here?"

"Out of town. Important business." So she was covering up, playing her part in the charade, even without knowing what had become of him. "My job to take care of this. Get our money back."

Paul made eye contact with J.T., who gave a quick nod. "Before you say any more, let me introduce myself. I'm Paul Kovacs from the Jersey City police department, this is Tom Kovacs, a criminal attorney, and this is J.T. Taylor, a detective with the NYPD." He didn't specify that J.T. was a homicide detective. That would just confuse things.

"We have your husband, your brother-in-law, his cousins, and his friends—the men in that picture—sitting in our jail as we speak. Part of the reason we're here is to figure out how many crimes to charge them with."

J.T. tapped the screen of his phone and said, "You've run this scam before. We've got the reports from Dallas and Chicago and San Francisco. Probably more coming. So, we'd like to ask you a few questions."

"I want to see my husband."

"No can do. He's in jail in another state, while you're a suspect right here," J.T. said, patting the table.

"Lawyer."

Tommy studied the ceiling as J.T. said, "Is that necessary? At this point we just want to ask you some questions. We can do that here or down at the precinct. If you have nothing to hide, why do you need a lawyer?"

"Lawyer!"

"Got my answer." He addressed Paul, "You done with me?"

"Sure am. Thanks for the help."

"No problem. Catch up with you later."

J.T. took the woman out, and they heard her loud complaints all the way down the hall.

"A word?" Williams asked his associate Long. They stepped into the hall and returned a moment later. "You have the ring?" Williams looked from Paul to Bert.

Bert fished the box out of his jacket pocket, opened it, and slid it across the table. "It's a beauty, all right."

"And now it has a story," Long said. "It survived the Great Korean Kidnapping Plot."

"What?"

"Think about the great stories. The Hope diamond, famous partly because Harry Winston sent it to the Smithsonian by U.S. mail. Think about the famous pearl earring King Charles I wore to his beheading."

"I'd rather not," Williams said.

"Emeralds gave Egyptian mummies trip insurance for the afterlife, and yellow diamonds, like this one—"

"Wait," interrupted Bert. "You mean that big stone is an actual diamond?" All the color drained from his face, and he looked like he might faint. "It was just in my pocket ..."

"Hindus associated yellow diamonds with Vishnu, god of the heavens. Reserved for only certain high-caste Indians. Our 128-carat yellow diamond created quite a sensation when Lady Gaga wore it to the Academy Awards. Part of its story is that it also was worn by Audrey Hepburn."

"I see an ad campaign coming," Williams, slightly shaking his head.

Long was warming up. "Our founder was called the 'King of Diamonds,' and now the king has escaped a brazen robbery attempt. It will be a great story!"

"Other thoughts?" Williams said, sounding hopeful.

Long excused himself and hurried out.

"No, I think we're done here," Tommy said. "Paul said all along their game was to get their hands on the ring. They thought buying it, then losing it, would make them the victims, not the perpetrators. One thing they didn't count on was Bert's total honesty. There was never a question that he'd find a way to bring it in."

"We appreciate that," Williams said, as Long returned, "more than you know. And, to show our appreciation and make amends for your losing your intended gift for—" he paused.

"His fiancée, Veronika," said Paul at the same time Bert said, "Hungarian Christmas."

"—we'd like you to have this instead." Williams held out the small box Long handed him.

Bert looked reluctant to take it.

"We insist," Williams said. "Picture?"

"Plus," said Long, getting a nice shot of a grinning Bert and the open box. "You've given me a great idea for a promotion. Hungarian Christmas. Next year for sure."

In the conference room, when Bert opened the box, he'd gasped, "Oh, I never—" and was hardly less delighted and astonished than Veronika was, several hours later.

She held out her right hand to admire the ring, a brilliant blue sapphire flanked by triangular diamonds.

"I have to tell you something, though." Bert said, "You won't believe this, but that yellow diamond—it was the real thing."

"The real thing, Bert?" Veronika embraced her future husband. "Just like you."

"Happy Hungarian Christmas."

ANOTHER BODY

Steve Beresford

Casey Baxter had already found more bodies than the average person. Well, sort of, anyway. And now she'd come across another, just lying there, it was, on the Delta P4 gantry.

Casey saw her first body from the river bridge in Malham Wood, but the approach through the undergrowth was too boggy and too treacherous for her to investigate further, so instead she called the emergency services. They arrived at speed and in considerable numbers. Unfortunately. Turned out the 'body' was merely some discarded clothes—probably tossed from the bridge by a litter lout for some reason— that had randomly shaped themselves like a sprawled bloodstained corpse. Casey's sense of duty was praised, if not her eyesight.

Her second discovery was at least a real body. A tramp, in the park. *Clearly* dead. Or so she thought when she checked, as would any concerned and dutiful citizen, for signs of life. The emergency services, however, managed quite easily to wake the derelict from his alcohol-induced stupor. Why he hadn't woken when Casey examined him she had no idea. She was remembered from her earlier find, and this time the appreciation of her good intentions was slightly more restrained.

The third time even Casey had to admit to some embarrassment. The woman was face-down in the canal, tangled in the weeds on the far bank, blonde hair rippling in the faint waves generated by the breeze. If only she hadn't been a shop mannequin the headlines could have been *so* different.

So Casey approached this new body—ostensibly her fourth—with some caution.

She'd been walking through the warehouse on an inspection, logging barcodes and tracking orders on her hand-held scanner. It was all computer-controlled, but Mr Hickman—who remained suspicious of the new multi-million-pound warehouse— liked her to spend a morning every week carrying out a manual check.

Casey hadn't heard anything, obviously, that might have brought about the appearance of a body here because she was wearing ear defenders to protect herself from the literally deafening noise of all the machinery. She wouldn't have heard a struggle had it been happening right behind her.

The warehouse itself was a miracle of engineering, an automated marvel that could pick, sort, merge, scan, pack and load various items without a single human hand interfering in the process at any point from storage site to back of the van. It was also like some mechanical, motorised version of hell, with all the clattering and banging and screeching as medical supplies of all descriptions shuttled automatically in bar-coded crates around the multi-level maze of conveyor belts and rollers.

She crouched by the prone figure on the gantry—Delta P4—laying down her hand-held scanner. Mere inches away crates trundled past towards the final packing stage.

This one was definitely a body. Dirty, stained jeans. Black Sabbath T-shirt beneath a black leather jacket. Untidy black hair. And a face only a mother could love. Pock-marked, scarred and stubbly. Most importantly, the body had no pass-card on a lanyard. And no ear defenders. Not staff then, nor a visitor. Intruder maybe? But definitely dead. She made sure after the debacle with the tramp in the park, checking repeatedly for a pulse and giving him a good shake. His eyes were glassy and unseeing too, having no doubt just stared into his killer's face. She noted the jacket, awkwardly off the shoulder, as if from a struggle, and also noted, with a slightly sick feeling, the knife embedded in his chest, surrounded by a small dark stain ...

Casey stood up abruptly, eyes frantically searching.

Killer.

It suddenly registered.

This wasn't an accident. And she'd been on this gantry just five minutes before. Which meant the body had appeared since then. Which meant his killer could still be close.

Her hand twitched instinctively to reach for her phone, but just as the clattering network of machinery would drown out any noise from a murderous struggle it would also smother her own appeals for help if she made a call. Not that calling was even possible. The network of surrounding metal effectively blocked phone signals too. Even a text message was impossible. So her hand froze as it touched the knitted pocket of her cardigan.

Then, a shadow, person-shaped. To her left. Although she could see no detail through the intervening ever-moving mechanisms.

She had to get out, had to reach safety.

Casey started walking, faster and faster with each step until she was running. Her shoe slipped at the next corner and she slammed hard into the computer console stationed there. Her phone slipped from her pocket and disappeared down into the innards between a gap in the gantry's grilled floor. DAMMIT! She went to run on, but found herself painfully yanked back to the console, as though by a hand at her neck. The touchscreen beeped several times and flashed ACCEPTED as, hands shaking in panic, she fought to untangle her pass-card and lanyard, which had somehow hooked around the scanner below the screen.

Then, down the steps, across the floor, dodging one of the automated trolleys, she hurtled into the nearest office and grabbed for the desk phone ...

Detective Inspector Mallory was not happy.

Casey had explained everything. Given him a description of the victim. Told him of her fear for her own life as she fled. But he didn't seem to believe her.

"A body?" Mallory scowled. He was a tall thin man with a cadaverous, humourless face and an ill-fitting suit. "Or maybe I should say: *another* body?"

They were upstairs in Eddie Cantrell's office, thankfully soundproofed, with a thick window that afforded a high-level panoramic view across the warehouse. Mallory's sergeant stood nearby, taking notes. Mr Hickman, her chubby boss, was there too, having driven over from Head Office some three miles away, and Eddie Cantrell, warehouse manager, now walked in, looking agitated. Other staff—drivers, loaders, engineers, etc.—were on the forecourt, away from the noise, giving statements.

The only person *not* around, apparently, was the poor guy who'd been stabbed. His body had, somehow, vanished. But where he'd gone was anyone's guess. And CCTV was no good. The security system was being upgraded and there was no coverage in and around the warehouse until Friday.

"A body?" said Mr Hickman. "Sounds highly improbable."

Casey was still breathing hard. "Section Delta P4." She pointed in the general direction. "I saw him. He'd been stabbed. In the chest."

"Stabbed." Inspector Mallory didn't sound convinced. "Right."

She remembered Mallory from the park, when she found the tramp who'd been, well, *pretending* to be dead. Mallory had made an appearance at the canal too, for the drowning mannequin. Neither time had he treated her with much respect or understanding.

"This is, what, your *fourth* now?" His mocking tone grated somewhat.

"Yes, but this time ..."

"*This time* there isn't even an actual body, real, plastic or otherwise. There are no signs of a struggle. No blood. No evidence of anything at all."

"I've been up there myself, Casey," said Eddie Cantrell, "showing the police around." He was in his shirtsleeves, Casey noticed, not his usual white warehouseman's coat, so his impressive physique was more noticeable. Under more normal, sane circumstances she often found him quite fanciable. "There's nothing," he continued. "Only your scanner on the gantry."

Yes, her scanner. She forgot to pick it up in her panicked escape from the gantry.

Eddie glanced towards the window again, as though checking on the progress of the investigation taking place. Eddie did care passionately about keeping his beloved warehouse running to a tight schedule and all this activity had to be aggravating him.

But Casey had more to worry about than the state of the warehouse. "I definitely saw a body. And there was someone else up there too, sneaking around." She remembered the lurking shadow. "That's why I got out of there so quickly."

"I have a strong urge to run you in for wasting police time," Mallory said. "Once is a mistake. Twice is a coincidence. *Three* times is ridiculous. But *four*? You're either attention-seeking or delusional. Or both. Or a lunatic."

"I know what I saw."

"What you *think* you saw."

"Is it possible," Mr Hickman said, "that this body wasn't dead? Perhaps he managed to stagger away somewhere after you left him."

"No, he was definitely dead."

"You thought the tramp was dead," said Mallory.

"The tramp didn't have a knife in his chest."

"A prank then," said Eddie Cantrell. "Fake knife, attached to his T-shirt somehow. These heavy metal nuts always take things too far. Someone knew you'd be up there and decided to play a cruel trick on you."

"I know … what … I SAW!" Casey was angry. No one was taking her seriously.

Inspector Mallory shook his head. "I'm going to call off the search. It's a complete waste of time and I shouldn't have let this farce go as far as it has." He directed his sergeant to round up the team and the man slipped out of the office. "I'm going to give you the benefit of the doubt, Miss Baxter, and assume that someone has organised a cruel prank because of your unfortunate history with discovering bodies everywhere you go." He pointed … pointedly. "But if I get one more call from you …"

He stalked out of the office, wincing at the assault on his ears as he stepped outside and trotted down the metal staircase.

Eddie Cantrell gestured after him. "I should really … Just in case …" And he nipped out too, closing the door behind him.

"Should have come to me first," Mr Hickman looked at her sadly, "before calling the police. We're lucky we didn't have to shut down. That could have thrown the schedules for the whole week. I mean … *a body*."

"There was!"

"A prank."

"No. And there was somebody else up there, Mr Hickman. Probably the murderer."

"I doubt it, Casey. It's so noisy and there's so much moving in every direction, casting weird shadows everywhere, that you could start believe anything was happening. It was probably some sort of brain overload."

"Are you calling me crazy?"

"No, no, not crazy. Over-worked maybe. Perhaps you need a holiday."

Holiday! The cheek of the man.

An hour later the police had all left, her phone had been found and returned to her, and Mr Hickman had gone back to Head Office. Casey, however, couldn't leave. Not yet. Because everything felt so … so *unresolved*. She stood on the raised walkway outside Eddie's office, leaning against the railing. The events of the day whirled in her fevered mind as she watched Eddie scurrying around.

Eddie had been up and down gantries and along walkways, peering here and there, checking that the police search team hadn't damaged his precious machinery. He clearly didn't believe her either.

Maybe she *had* imagined it. Even with her ear defenders back on the noise was awful, enough to send the sanest person a little doolally. Unless it *was* a prank, as Eddie suggested, with the knife somehow attached through the C of the Black Sabbath design of the body's …

Casey frowned.

She watched Eddie, still coat-less, emerging from a maintenance crawl-space beneath the machinery. No. It was unthinkable, surely. But …

She hurried into his office, closing the door and removing her ear defenders.

It didn't take much searching before she found his white warehouseman's coat stuffed in the bottom of his filing cabinet. She flattened it out across his desk. He was wearing it when she arrived earlier that morning, before all the hoo-ha started. And he *always* wore it. So why wasn't he wearing it now?

Eddie was almost fanatical about his coat. Treated it like some sort of religious vestment. He washed and tumble-dried it almost every night and had been known to explode if it got marked or stained. But the pocket was ripped, the stitching torn, the material crumpled—as if someone had grabbed it hard. In a struggle maybe.

And there, on the cuff. A splash of red. Tiny, though. Like a single squirt of … of blood.

Holy sugar! Casey had to remind herself to breathe.

Apart, they were nothing. Even together—the rip and the stain—they didn't add up to much. But taken together with …

The door opened suddenly and Eddie burst in, the cacophony of the warehouse spilling in around him.

"Oh!" He stared at her, then closed the door. "I didn't realise you were still …" He saw his coat, laid out on his desk. "What are you …"

"How did you know about the guy's T-shirt, Eddie?" Casey said.

"T-shirt?"

"When you said it might be a prank, you mentioned the guy was wearing a T-shirt. You even talked about him being a heavy metal nut." Black Sabbath were heavy metal, weren't they? "But you weren't there when I gave his description to Inspector Mallory. So how did you know?" It was a simple question, with a simple answer: *I heard it from someone.* But instead Eddie looked terrified.

"I … I … I …"

"And why is your pocket ripped? And is this blood?"

"Casey, look …" Eddie visibly deflated. "I didn't mean to do it. But he came at me. With a knife. And we fought. And he dropped the knife. And I picked it up. And he came at me again. I had no choice really. It was kill or be killed."

"So there *was* a body? How come you didn't say anything?"

"What? And admit to murder? Be serious, Casey!"

Casey was feeling pretty serious. "Hold on, who *was* this guy? What was he doing here?"

"He's called Frank. Frank Owen. He's a complete nutjob. And I've been … Well, I've been having an affair with his wife. He must have found out because he turned up here this morning. Said he wanted to kill me and he pulled out a knife. I ran off, hoping I could lose him in the gantries and sneak back out to my car. But somehow he cornered me in Packing. Then we fought. And then you turned up. And so I hid, just in time."

"Why didn't you own up and claim self-defence?"

"I panicked."

Eddie was still panicking. Twitching and shuddering.

"Then, when you ran away," he said, "I nipped off, grabbed a trolley and loaded him into it. I thought if I could get him out of the building somehow … But on the stairs I lost control of the trolley and it tipped over. And he fell out. And sort of slipped through the workings. I thought he fell into a crate, but when I got down there he'd gone. Then all hell broke lose after you called for help and I had to stop searching." He put his hands to his head, as though worried his brain was about to explode and crack his skull open. "I'm pretty sure now he couldn't have been dead. He must have come round and wandered off. That's why I've been searching. He could be lying somewhere. You have to help me, Casey. You know me. I'm a good man. I didn't mean to stab him. So if I could just find him, and finish him off if I need to, and hide him properly ... I'd be safe. Help me find him, Casey. Help me. Please."

Panicked *and* crackers now.

"But the police would have found him if he were still here," she said.

"You think so?" Eddie frowned. It was quite possible he was losing his mind completely. Perhaps this was what working every day in this cacophonous hell-hole did to a person. Your brain just melted. "Not if he kept moving around and hiding."

So that's why Eddie had been mooching through the innards of the warehouse. He was searching, not checking.

Casey wondered if she needed to go on a first aid course or something like that— because she clearly found it difficult to tell whether someone was actually dead or not. You can find a pulse in the neck, can't you? After all, if this Frank Owen *had* been dead then the police ought to have spotted him easily. But her thoughts on that matter were cut short, because Eddie was reaching for the door handle again.

"Come on, Casey," he said. "Help me look for him." He flung open the door, noise flooding in around him like a physical force.

"No! Wait!"

He paused, looked back.

"I can't help you," she said.

He frowned. "WHAT?"

"I CAN'T ..." Casey darted forward and grabbed his wrist. "YOU NEED TO ..."

"LET GO." Eddie yanked his arm away.

"EDDIE! PLEASE."

"BUT I CAN STILL ..." He backed away from her, along the high walkway, towards the metal staircase leading down to the main floor.

"NO, EDDIE. I'M GOING TO CALL THE ..."

"... THE POLICE? YOU CAN'T. THEY'LL ..."

"I HAVE TO." She reached for him again.

Eddie flinched back beyond her grasp, turning to go down the staircase behind him, but he misjudged how close he was and his foot landed awkwardly on the top step, toppling him sideways, then forwards.

Casey screamed when she realised what was happening.

And Eddie disappeared, head-first, down the metal staircase, arms flailing, hands grasping uselessly …

Inspector Mallory stood by the black van as Eddie Cantrell's lifeless form was loaded into the back.

"Yet another body. This makes five now, that you've called about." He shook his head in disbelief. "So he fell?"

"Eddie just lost his balance," Casey said. "In his mad rush." Broken neck was the preliminary verdict from the pathologist.

Mallory frowned. "And there really was a body then? Earlier?"

"I did say."

"You claimed he was dead."

"Well, yes." She'd told Mallory all about Frank Owen and Eddie's part in the man's stabbing. And reluctantly she had to admit that Mr Owen may not have been dead after all. She *had* been wrong before. After being tipped unceremoniously into the machinery the injured man must have somehow slipped away unseen.

"I'll widen the search area, now we know he's gone walkabout. He'll probably need emergency treatment, if we can find him in time." He looked at Casey. "And you …" pointing seriously "… don't find any more bodies. Okay? Or if you do, don't call me."

Casey eventually went home—hot bath, cool bottle of wine—only returning to her desk at Head Office the following day to continue with her usual duties. An email was waiting on her computer—an order confirmation for medical supplies.

An order? She frowned. *From her own company?*

Then she remembered running away from the body yesterday and banging into the computer station on the gantry. Her pass-card had got wrapped around the scanner there and she'd accidentally pressed her hands against the touchscreen. ACCEPTED, it had displayed. And apparently the system had overwritten the original delivery address—a Tamworth hospital, according to the order history—with her own office address from the database.

"Hey, Casey." The voice came across the open-plan office. "There's a delivery for you. At reception."

"Coming."

A shiver of terrible anticipation tickled her spine. No, it couldn't be. She hurried down to reception to find a large box waiting for her. One of the company's delivery boxes. Transported the three miles from warehouse to Head Office.

She borrowed scissors to slice the seal and flipped back the lid. And there, amongst the polystyrene chips, was the face of a dead man. Frank Owen.

Someone screamed behind her, but Casey could easily believe it, with her track record.

Eddie reckoned the man had slipped away, injured, but still alive, after falling into the machinery, but Casey had known he was dead. *She'd known.*

Instead he must have dropped into a crate, a crate heading for Packing, and the automated system had reassessed the weight and size and upgraded the packaging to something more suitable, then shipped it out to the amended address.

Computers, eh?

"You'd better call the police." She sighed. "And ask for Inspector Mallory."

He wouldn't be happy.

Constantly coming across bodies was one thing …

… but now she was having them delivered.

SANTA WALKS INTO A BAR

Frank Oreto

"Santa Claus walks into a bar," Paul said the words slowly. An opener like that and you have them smiling right away. People know a zinger is coming. Except Paul didn't have a punchline, and after ten years he didn't think one was forthcoming.

He got lucky and found an empty parking space right across from Drake's Bar and Grill. The official-police-business placard on the visor let him ignore the parking meter. Paul's business tonight was about as personal as you could get, but being a cop should have its perks.

In a few hours, college students would fill East Carson Street for one more night of debauchery before heading home for Christmas with the family. It was early though, only six p.m. and relatively quiet. Of course, you could still find trouble if you went looking for it. Paul wasn't looking for trouble. He was looking for a skinny, bald probation officer named Ivan Guskov and he knew where to find him.

Ivan sat on the same barstool as always. He wore his usual monkey-brown corduroy blazer with a green plaid scarf looped about his thin neck. He looked over his shoulder as Paul walked toward the bar and his face broke into a wide grin. Paul knew from that smile he was right on time.

They'd become friends through work and bad habits. Paul helped bring in a few of Ivan's clients over the years, and they discovered gambling and drinking were pastimes they both appreciated more than they should. These days, Paul might still put fifty down on the Steelers, but he'd given up the booze. He had Ivan to thank for that.

Paul took a seat and stared into the gold-flecked mirror behind the bar. Ivan sat beside him, looking out of place with no drink. They made an odd pair. Ivan's hatchet face and narrow frame contrasting with Paul's coarse pugilist's features and linebacker shoulders—a run-down Laurel next to a Hardy gone savage.

The bartender looked barely old enough to drink. Paul hadn't seen him before. It wasn't surprising. Paul only came by once a year.

"Um ... you're Paul Drazdzinski, right?" The bartender asked, sounding flustered. "Mr. Drake said you were um—" He swallowed and tried again. "So, what'll you have?"

Paul smiled like only a twenty-five-year-on-the-job cop could. The bartender flinched. "What's your name, kid?"

"Eddie, Eddie Donneley."

"And you obviously know who I am."

"Yes, sir. Mr. Drake described you. Said you'd be here tonight."

"Where is the boss? I didn't think he ever left."

"Helen, his wife, she's not doing real well. You know, the cancer."

Paul had not known but nodded anyway. "Give me a Jamison's neat and some cranberry juice on the rocks." When the drinks came, Paul slid the whiskey in front of Ivan and took a sip of the cranberry juice.

"So, you're the guy—" Eddie started.

Paul cut him off. "Listen, I'm not here to relive old times or tell you a funny story." The kid flinched again. Paul felt bad. "It's okay." He pulled a twenty out of his wallet and laid it on the bar. "I just want to rent a couple of stools for about ..." He looked at his watch. "Another twenty-five minutes or so. I don't want any conversation. We'll be fine."

Eddie glanced toward where Ivan sat and back to Paul. Then he nodded and walked away.

Ivan laughed silently, his shoulders bobbing.

Paul took another sip from his glass and cut his eyes toward Ivan. "Okay, so maybe I am here to relive the past." The cranberry juice had a bite, but not the kind Paul craved. "Isn't it time for you to take a piss, you degenerate-gambler."

Ivan slid off the barstool and headed for the can. He threw back an insult that Paul couldn't hear followed by a hand gesture he understood just fine.

Eddie, the bartender, pulled a pitcher of Yuengling and glanced nervously at Paul in the mirror.

Paul thought about smiling at him again but didn't want to make the poor kid cry. Besides, He seemed nice enough. Paul sometimes wished he and Maggie's marriage had a child to show for it, instead of just painful memories and a divorce decree. *I'd have probably screwed that up too*, he thought. Paul shook his head, imagining a houseful of kids that flinched when their old man smiled.

"What the hell," he said under his breath. He had some time to kill, and Ivan sure wouldn't mind. *Call it a bedtime story for all the ones I never got to tell.* He motioned to Eddie.

"So, you want to hear about what happened?"

The bartender nodded. He looked unsure but curious.

Ivan slid back onto the barstool but only had eyes for the flat screen mounted on the wall. Some reality show was on. Pretty, vacuous people behaving badly.

"Hey, could you change the channel to ESPN?" Paul asked.

Eddie did.

"Okay then, it was ten years ago. Santa Claus walks into a bar. That was me. We'd got the suit from Onstage Costumes, the big shop down in the Strip. They'd been robbed over Halloween, and we caught the bad guys. Hell, we even found the money, and that doesn't happen often. So, they wanted to give us something. We're not allowed to accept gifts, but we do this Toys-for-Tots thing every Christmas, and the costume got written up as a donation to the program. It was a nice one, real-looking beard and one of those foam-fat suits like they wear in the movies.

"I volunteered to take it on a test run. Walked around the station, Ho Ho Ho-ing, giving away "get out of jail free cards" to the bad guys. So, I thought, let the good times roll, and took my show on the road. Ivan and me, we had a standing engagement here most Monday nights to get drunk and watch a game. I thought I'd give him a laugh.

"The crowd ate it up. Women wanted to sit on my lap. People kept asking why they didn't get what they wanted for Christmas last year.

"There was this one guy though, playing pool by himself in the corner. He kept staring at me. Big fella. My size, but fat. Decked out for the holidays in faded jeans and a dirty flannel shirt. I didn't know what his problem was. Maybe he'd gotten a few too many lumps of coal as a kid. But screw him, right? Everybody else was having a good time.

"So, we drank and we talked. I told Ivan how my wife turned off the radio every time 'Baby It's Cold Outside' came on. Said it was too rapey. Ivan said all Christmas carols were about rape if you examined the subtext. Funny guy, right?" Paul looked over at Ivan. "Weird, but funny."

"Anyway, the guy who'd been giving me the hairy eyeball walks by. I figured he's hitting the can, but he stops and stares at me, opening and closing his mouth like a landed trout. He finally jerks a thumb at his chest and says, 'My name's Andy Swafford,' like it's supposed to mean something. Then he says, 'Screw you, Kris Kringle,' turns around, and walks back to the pool tables. The funny thing was how serious he was. Like I'd been putting the old Yule log to his mom every Christmas for years, and he finally had enough.

"Ivan, he about busts a gut laughing. But you know, I got mad. Like the jerk had disrespected the uniform. You just don't talk that way to Santa."

Eddie grinned. Paul nodded at him. "It's funny, right? Even though you know how bad it's gonna turn out, you still got to laugh.

"So, I walked to the pool table and watched the guy try to sink the seven ball and screw it up. He didn't notice me at first. Then he froze up and turned around real slow, his eyes getting wider and wider.

"I should have noticed something. The crazy ones have a smell. But I was up four shots of bourbon by then, so I stood there grinning as he dropped the pool cue and pulled the pistol from his waistband.

"He fired three shots. No one ever shot me before. I kept thinking; this isn't so bad. It doesn't even hurt. We stood there looking at each other. I guess we were both waiting for me to fall down. But I didn't."

"It was the fat suit, right?" said Eddie.

I shook my head. "Good guess, kid, but memory foam ain't Kevlar. He just missed. Five feet away and that jag-off misses all three shots. A Christmas freakin' miracle. When I realized I didn't have a bullet in me, all the fear of dying changed into this mix of relief and rage. I laughed.

"Swafford still held the weapon, but he didn't seem to know what to do with it anymore. I got close, twisted his wrist, and the gun slid across the floor. Then I took the guy apart.

"I went slow. I wanted to do more than hurt the guy. I wanted to humiliate him. Hit him with big open-hand slaps across the face, hard enough make him stagger. He started blubbering, which only pissed me off more.

"You'd a thought somebody would call the cops. They didn't though. Maybe it was all too weird. Santa gets shot at then beats the crap out of the shooter. People weren't panicking, they were laughing. Started yelling stuff like, 'Kick his ass, Nick,' and 'Dude's definitely naughty.' Some of them cheered.

"I got into it. Hamming it up for the crowd. 'You better not pout.' Followed by a slap across the face. 'You better not cry'—crack! Then I pulled him in close enough that the blood dripped from his split-open lips onto my white beard. " 'And you sure as hell better never ever shoot at Santa Claus.'

"This time my hand was a fist, with all my weight plus a whole lot of drunken anger behind it. I felt the shooter's nose collapse. Blood sprayed as he hit the floor, out cold. I picked up the gun and turned around to face the crowd, hands in the air like I'd won a prizefight. Funny right?"

Eddie wasn't laughing. He looked a little sick.

Paul nodded. "Yeah, I screwed up."

Eddie shook his head. "It wasn't your fault. The guy shot at you. You weren't thinking straight."

Paul glanced at his watch, then turned from the bartender to Ivan. "It was my fault. I'm a cop." Paul still spoke to the bartender, but the words were for Ivan, apologizing. Again. "It was my job to subdue the shooter. I had cuffs in my pocket. It should have taken three seconds. Take the gun, face down on the pool table, hands cuffed. Instead, I put on a God-damned show."

Ivan stared through Paul toward the empty pool tables.

"If I'd done my job, I'd have put down the shooter and looked to see where the bullets went."

As Paul watched, his old friend's head jerked slightly to the side. Ivan reached up to the scarf knotted around his neck. His hand came away wet with dark blood.

"You're seeing him now, aren't you?" asked Eddie.

"Shut up kid."

Ivan tried to stand but sagged back onto the barstool. No one noticed when it happened ten years ago. Least of all Paul as he laughed and beat the head case into bloody gristle. No one wondered where the bullets had landed.

Ivan looked down at the blood on his hand as if he couldn't figure out how it got there. He coughed a red cloud that would have speckled Paul's white shirt with bloody dots if Ivan had really been there. He clawed at the bar for a moment, trying to find some purchase. A way to push himself up. He couldn't do it. Instead, Ivan's head sank onto the cool wood as if he needed to take a little nap before giving it another try.

Paul didn't witness Ivan Guskov's death that night. No one had. The first person to notice was the woman tending bar. She screamed when she saw the blood pooled around Ivan's head. By then, he'd been gone for minutes.

A year later—a year of drinking and telling the department-appointed therapist to go to hell—Paul came back to Drake's, already drunk, to find Ivan sitting at the same barstool. Paul stood there for a while, yelling and waving his hand through the empty air before he finally sat down next to his friend and ordered a drink. It was a miracle they served him.

That night, for the first time, Paul watched Ivan die. He'd been there every year since. Bearing witness to the passing of the friend he'd let down and vowing he would always know where the bullets ended up.

Paul's sight blurred from unshed tears. When he wiped them away, Ivan's barstool was empty.

"Jesus, you saw him didn't you, the guy who died?" Eddie asked. His voice was high with excitement.

"No, I didn't see a damn thing," said Paul. He held up his tumbler of cranberry juice and motioned toward the shot of whiskey with his eyes. "To Ivan Guskov."

Eddie picked up the whiskey. "To Ivan."

They drank.

Paul set his glass down and laid another twenty on the bar. "Merry Christmas, kid," he said and walked out into the cold Pennsylvania night.

THE X IN XMAS

Robert Jeschonek

Multicolored Christmas lights blink and flicker at night in the snowy central park of the town of Abruzzi, Pennsylvania. The decorations don't inspire the slightest twinkle of Christmas spirit in Detective Charlie Collins, Abruzzi P.D.

Fat white flakes flutter down, clinging to Charlie's black overcoat and melting fast against his dark brown skin. Snapping on latex gloves, he prowls the gazebo in the heart of the park, focused on the ugliness amid the holiday beauty. All he cares about is the crime scene in the gazebo, complete with a dead Santa Claus in a sleigh.

Charlie's dark eyes scan for details with practiced intensity, seeking out any telling traces beyond the obvious ... which is to say, the bearded Caucasian man in the sleigh took a bullet to the brain. That, however, is not the only major detail that jumps out at Charlie and his partner.

"Since when does Santy Claus dress in black?" asks middle-aged, beer-bellied Officer Burt Sichak, who was the first law enforcement on the scene.

It's a good question. The dead man's clothes look like standard Santa-wear, except for the fact that they're all pitch black. Even the fur trim and hat tassel, which are usually white, are full-on black.

"You ever seen a Santa outfit like that, Charlie?" Burt looks like a rotten potato in a parka, and his cheeks are flushed from drinking. He was off-duty when the body turned up. "What does the African-American Saint Nick wear?"

Charlie ignores him. Burt's sense of humor sometimes leans toward racism; his comments don't always sit well with Charlie, and he doesn't seem to care how Charlie takes them.

Things were different in Charlie's hometown of Pittsburgh ... but the 'Burgh, which is two hours south, might as well be a world away. Charlie's been in Abruzzi since his fortieth birthday six months ago, and he's learned to pick his battles. He's nobody's fool, but he doesn't dial it up to eleven all the time either.

The job is what matters most to him, as awful as it gets ... and tonight's brutal murder is pretty awful. "Looks like a mob hit. Tap to the back of the head, exit wound up front."

Burt snickers. "Santa picked the wrong goombah to give a lump a' coal to, I guess."

Charlie nods. It's a fact of life; the Mafia's been a force in Abruzzi forever. This part of the state is thick with them.

Something catches Charlie's eye then, and he leans closer to the corpse. There's a crumpled bit of paper in Santa's fist, and he works to pry it out. It looks like the edges are torn, as if someone ripped the rest of it free but couldn't get the last shred from Santa's death grip.

Charlie can't get the last shred either. He finally gives up and searches Santa's pockets, which is where he finds a battered black leather wallet. There's a driver's license inside, which he slides out for a better look.

"We've got a tentative I.D. on the vic," he says. "According to this, the ex-Santa Claus is one Dominick Rialto."

"Hey, that's the produce guy," says Burt.

"Owner of Sunshine Market, right?"

"Also old school Black Hand Mafia," Burt says solemnly. "No *wonder* his Santy suit is all black!"

Charlie frowns. "Is that a thing?"

"It was for Dominick," says Burt. "Black Hand was started by Italian immigrants and evolved into the Mafia we got now. I've heard stories how hardcore it was. Dominick used to say he was part of it back in the day."

"Black Hand Mafia." Charlie nods. "Black costume Santa Claus. I wonder if they're connected."

"Old school guy in his 70s like that, maybe he wanted to pay tribute to the Black Hand with his outfit." Burt smirks and shrugs. "Or maybe he just thought it was funny, who knows?"

"But was it enough for someone to make him an *ex*-Santa?" asks Charlie. "Maybe the note in his hand will clear things up."

"My money's on a reindeer takin' down this guy." Burt nods knowingly. "I never did trust that Rudolph. Red nose can be a sign of alcohol abuse, y'know."

"What do you have for me, Peg?" Charlie sweeps into the morgue at 6 a.m. on Christmas Eve day like he's not running on coffee and zero sleep.

Peg Wonders, county coroner, holds up a sealed evidence baggie with a wrinkled scrap of paper inside. "He's makin' a list … and checkin' it twice …" She swings the baggie back and forth between her thumb and forefinger as she sings. "Gonna find out who's ... *naughty!*"

Charlie smiles. Peg has a way of cracking him up. "Well, well." He takes the baggie from her and holds it up to the light to make out the five partial lines of handwriting on the paper inside. "What kind of list is this?"

"Mafioso Santa's, apparently." Peg, in her 50s and full of attitude, puffs a strand of gray hair away from her right eye. "No dollies or bicycles on *that* list."

Charlie moves the paper closer. It's only three inches by two inches at its most intact point, and the handwritten lines are mostly fragments.

" 'Tony Petrilli.' " He reads the first line aloud, what there is of it. "Then a dash. Then 'OxyContin, 100 tabs,' with the second half of the letter 's' cut off."

"We know what *that* is," Peg says glibly as she cleans the blade of a rotary bone saw.

"Lonnie DeGol." The start of the second line is visible, though more of the end is missing. "Then a dash, followed by 'Guns and ammo.' "

"A friend of the N.R.A., no doubt," says Peg.

"On the next line, we have the name 'Vito Arcurio.' Beside that, we have the entry 'Persian rug.' "

Peg frowns. "Someone in the floor covering trade?"

"Next line starts with the partial last name 'vino.' Then a dash, followed by 'Escalade.' And that's it."

"Wish we knew who 'vino' is." Peg frowns.

"So how did they use this list, exactly?" asks Charlie. "Did the mobsters line up to sit on Black Hand Santa's knee?"

" 'We've been bad boys this year, Santa. As a reward, we want drugs, guns, a rug, and a fancy new car for Xmas, please.' " Peg laughs and pulls back the sheet from the body on the table. "I guess Dominick here had his own holiday traditions, huh?"

"What else did you find?" asks Charlie.

"Food and wine stains on the outfit. No surprise there. Cigar ash too. Also traces of some kind of lotion or ointment around the neck."

"Ointment?"

"I'm sending it out for analysis. Otherwise, aside from the *obvious* ..." She gestures at the remnants of Dominick's exploded head. "... just another overweight, diabetic mobster in his 70s with knee, hip, and shoulder replacements and a big fat belly that shook like a bowl full of—"

"Excuse me." A woman knocks once and pushes the door open. "Hello?"

She instantly has Charlie's attention, and not just because she shouldn't be down here unescorted.

"I'll be damned." She spots the body on the slab and shakes her head sadly. "So that's all that's left of Dominick Rialto?"

The woman is in her thirties and has long, dark hair and an athletic build. She wears a black leather jacket, a black sweater, and jeans. Charlie is instantly intrigued and notices the absence of a wedding ring. "Excuse me," he says. "I'll have to ask you to step outside, Miss ..."

"Malditesta," says the dark-haired woman. "Detective Marie Malditesta of the Allegheny County Organized Crime Task Force, based in Pittsburgh."

"Hello." Charlie hasn't met her before, but he recognizes her name from his Pittsburgh days. "You came because of Dominick?" He gestures at the corpse.

"I drove up as soon as I heard," says Marie. "Mr. Rialto and I have history, you see. He was one of my informants the past couple of years."

"You're shittin' me," says Burt, who just appeared in the doorway behind her. "Dominick Rialto was a *rat?*"

Marie clears her throat and gives Charlie a look. "Can we go somewhere and have a chat, Detective ...?"

"Collins." Charlie smiles back at her. "Detective Charlie Collins. And yes, right this way." He walks her past Burt and out the door ... though Burt follows them, determined to stay in the mix.

The three of them—Charlie, Marie, and Burt—sit across from each other at the big metal table in the interview room, nursing coffees.

"So here's the thing, Detective." Marie's accent has a hint of Long Island to it. "I want to help you find out who did this to Mr. Rialto."

"How do you propose to do that?" asks Charlie.

"I know some people because of the task force," says Marie. "I might be able to open some doors for you."

"Maybe so." With that, Charlie gets up from the table, signals with his index finger that he'll only be gone a moment, and leaves the room. He soon returns carrying the fragment of paper in the evidence baggie. "So what can you tell me about this? And the whole black Santa getup?"

"Yeah," says Burt. "What's with the whole *Clausa Nostra* thing?" He cracks himself up with the joke.

Marie reads the scrap in the bag and raises an eyebrow. "You found this on Mr.

Rialto?"

"We did," says Charlie. "So it *is* a thing, then?"

"It's a thing. I've heard about this."

"Meaning what?" asks Burt.

"Meaning the local goombahs have Christmas parties like everyone else," says Marie. "With *presents.*"

"Presents from Santy Claus?" says Burt.

"From the boss, at least," says Marie. "They call it Bonus Night. On Bonus Night, the lieutenants get to ask for a Christmas bonus for all their hard work during the year."

"And the boss just gives it to them?" asks Burt.

She shrugs. "As long as they've been bad little boys, I suppose."

"Any idea where they have this Bonus Night get-together?" asks Charlie.

"As a matter of fact, I do," says Marie. "It's right here in town, and it's a very Christmasy setting, in a manner of speaking ... one that's owned by the first guy on your list, as a matter of fact."

Was the Christ child born in Italy? You might think so from looking around the entryway of Petrilli's Ristorante in Abruzzi.

As the maître d' ushers Marie, Charlie, and Burt into the place, they pass a painting of the Nativity set in the heart of St. Peter's Square in the Vatican. A little further along the entryway, a lighted plastic Nativity rests in a corner, an Italian flag draped behind it. Then there's the framed photo of a live Nativity staged in a gondola in a canal in Venice, occupying a lighted niche just before the last turn into the dining room.

Charlie's used to it all, he's been here before ... but it still strikes him as more tacky than charming. Most of the restaurant's clientele see it the other way around, though. The cheesy decorations have been around for so long, Petrilli's regulars feel downright nostalgic about them.

The maître d' says he'll fetch the owner and disappears through the kitchen door. That leaves Charlie with time to look around the dining room and appreciate the more classic decorations in there. The place isn't open for lunch yet, so there aren't any customers blocking the view.

The dining room is strung with strands of white lights, boughs of fir and holly, and sprigs of mistletoe. Wreaths with red velvet bows line the walls, and red and green tablecloths alternate across the room. Then there's the tree in the far corner, tastefully hung with glittering ornaments, tinsel, lights, and tufts of simulated snow. Tucked between the base of the tree and the wall, Charlie sees a three-foot-long pine box with three softball-sized lights mounted on it—one green, one amber, and one red. Is the box dark because the bulbs are burned out, or is it not plugged in for some reason?

Suddenly, a mustached, barrel-chested man in a dark suit emerges from the kitchen. His black hair is slicked back on his head, and he looks about fifty something. Charlie has seen him around but never met him before today.

"I own this place." His voice is low and gravelly. "Whadda you want?"

"I'm Detective Charlie Collins." Charlie walks over and extends a hand, but the guy doesn't take the shake, so he nods at Marie. "This is Detective Marie Malditesta of the Organized Crime Task Force. And this ..."

"Yo, Tony." Burt gives him a nod. "How's it hangin'?"

Tony Petrilli shrugs. "So what can I do you for?"

"First off, congratulations on your Christmas bonus." Charlie pulls out a copy of Black Hand Santa's list and holds it up. "I mean, a hundred tabs of OxyContin, that's not bad."

Tony snorts. "I don't know what you're talkin' about."

"Or maybe it wasn't enough," offers Marie. "Maybe that's why you killed him."

"Killed who?" Tony sneers.

"Dominick Rialto," says Burt. "He was found dead last night."

Tony hardly looks surprised. "Izzat so?" He frowns. "Last I saw, he was alive *right here*." He points at the floor. "Playin' Santa at the Italian Heritage Society's Christmas party."

"So you *were* one of the last people to see him alive," says Marie.

"Me and a hundred other guys, sure!" snaps Tony. "Plus wait staff!"

"But you were right *in* there, weren't you?" says Charlie. "Telling Santa what you wanted for Christmas. And then Lonnie DeGol was right behind you ..."

"And Vito Arcurio after him," adds Marie.

"What the *hell* are you *talkin'* about?"

"We're talking about murdering Santa after he didn't give you what you wanted," says Burt.

"Hey!" Indignant, Tony gets in his face. "Santa was perfectly *alive* when he walked out that door!" He points toward the exit.

"Okay," says Charlie. "So when did Dominick leave the party, exactly?"

"I don't remember!" Tony's face turns redder by the minute. "Maybe 10, maybe 11?"

"And when did *you* leave?"

"After everyone else straggled out of here. Like two in the morning. Long freakin' night, know what I mean?"

"Not so long for Dominick though," says Burt.

"What about Lonnie and Vito?" asks Charlie.

"Lonnie hauled ass right after Dominick," says Tony. "I remember Dominick forgot his hat, and Lonnie ran it out to him."

"And Vito?" asks Charlie.

"How the hell should I know?" snaps Tony. "I wasn't his *date.*"

"What about this other name on the list?" asks Charlie. "Something ending in -vino."

"Wow, *that* narrows it down," says Tony. "To like *half* the guys here."

"Do you have a guest list?" asks Charlie.

"For a party like *that*?" Tony laughs. "Sure, and I've got *selfies* with all the boys to go with it!"

After talking to Tony, the team splits up, with Charlie and Marie going to interview Lonnie DeGol while Burt heads over to search Dominick's house in the suburbs.

Finding Lonnie's a problem at first, since he's an out-of-town guy. That's where Marie makes a difference. A call to a colleague on the task force gets her the number of an undercover contact. The contact texts her an address where Lonnie might be staying in town, and they're off and running.

Unfortunately, when they get there—a dump of an apartment on the bad side of Abruzzi—Lonnie isn't around ... just a blonde girlfriend who claims he went home to Erie.

"Shit." Marie flicks Lonnie's mug shot on the dash. "Never had this problem with my *last* snitch." She means Dominick. "Something tells me I'm not gonna make it home to Pittsburgh for Midnight Mass tonight."

"Midnight Mass is a big deal for you?" asks Charlie.

"Pretty big," says Marie. "I sing with the choir. First soprano. I'm a soloist."

"Well, maybe you can still make it. Let's move to the next guy on the list and see how it goes," says Charlie. "We've got a local address for Vito Arcurio, so let's head over there. Maybe we can get someone to pick up Lonnie in Erie after that."

It turns out they don't need to wait to find Lonnie, after all. When Charlie and Marie roll up to Vito's house, Lonnie's running out the front door with a pistol in his hand. Vito tears out after him with his own gun, taking shots at him.

But when they see Charlie and Marie getting out of their unmarked car in the driveway, they instantly lose interest in each other and run off in separate directions.

Charlie and Marie don't say a word. Charlie bolts after Lonnie, and Marie follows Vito, drawing their weapons as they race like track stars through the neighbors' yards.

"Freeze!" Even as he shouts the word, Charlie knows it's a futile gesture. Lonnie's got a big head start and shows no sign of slowing down.

Not to mention, he's young and athletic enough to stay out ahead. His feet hammer through the grass like pistons, propelling him further out of reach.

Lucky for Charlie, the punk isn't immune to twists of fate. Just as Lonnie crosses a driveway a couple houses up, the reckless teen driver who lives there guns his parents' car out of the garage, clipping him good. Lonnie bounces off the tail end of the Toyota and goes down like a sack of dirt on the pavement.

Before Lonnie can jump back up, Charlie's on top of him, rolling him over on his belly. As soon as he's got the cuffs on his wrists, Charlie retrieves the hood's .9-mil from the grass.

"Hey, Lonnie," he says. "I need to ask you a few questions, *capiche?*"

Lonnie might have had the edge when it came to outrunning Charlie, but Marie has the advantage over Vito. She's a marathoner, built for speed and trained like a thoroughbred for championship racing. It doesn't hurt that she's wearing black sneakers as she always does on duty, for just such a perp-chasing occasion.

She's on Vito's heels in nothing flat. Vito has no athletic skill to speak of and quickly feels her breath on the back of his neck.

Which is why he suddenly swings the pistol back and randomly pulls the trigger.

Marie sees it coming in a split-second and ducks the shot. Before he can take another, she bashes his hand with her own sidearm, sending his gun hurtling out of his grip.

Then, with a cry of exertion, she pounces. Like a lion taking down a gazelle, she tackles Vito to the ground where he belongs.

"Time to talk, you piece of garbage!" She rolls him around and breaks out the cuffs. "What did you do to Dominick Rialto?"

Charlie and Marie put the suspects in the car and haul them back to the police station. They set them up one at a time in the interview room and pepper them with questions—but nobody's talking.

"So much for giving gifts on Christmas Eve," says Charlie.

Then, Marie has an idea. She tells Charlie she'll be right back, and then she goes for a brief drive.

When she returns, she has Tony Petrilli in tow for a trumped-up unpaid traffic ticket beef. She makes a point of marching him through the squad room, uncuffed, just as Charlie (at a prearranged signal) brings Vito through on the scenic route from the interview room to his cell.

Tony doesn't look his way, but Vito turns pale. By the time he leaves the room, however, his face is beet red.

Marie and Charlie both notice. Until now, they were only playing a hunch, but the hunch has been confirmed. Tony and Vito are both involved in the murder.

Lonnie's involved, too, apparently. His expressions are almost identical to Vito's when Charlie marches him through the squad room past Tony.

The next time they have their respective sit-downs, the two wiseguys are suddenly more talkative. Tony still hasn't said a word, but Vito and Lonnie both think he has, and Charlie and Marie encourage their misconception. The resulting chats are quite revealing.

The note in Santa's fist, for example, wasn't at all what Charlie thought it was.

"Every year on Bonus Night, Santa Dominick made a list of what all the fellas asked for," says Lonnie, "but that list you got ain't it."

"*Santa* didn't make *that* list," explains Vito.

"The four of *us* did," says Lonnie.

"That's right," says Vito. "Me, Lonnie, Tony, and one other guy."

"You better hurry if you want *that* guy, though," says Lonnie. "If I know that back-crackin' bastard, he'll be blowin' outta town the second he hears you've got the rest of us."

Burt backs up what Charlie and Marie just heard. Out at Dominick's place, his search turned up a product—*lots* of it—that's only sold one place in town. The lab confirms the product's a match for the residue on Dominick's neck.

And there's another thing. According to Lonnie and Vito, Dominick was dead or most of the way there *before* he got shot. There was a *second* murder weapon, one that Charlie spotted without realizing what it was during his first visit to Tony Petrilli's restaurant.

Charlie remembers it as plain as day—a three-foot pine box with red, green, and amber lights. It caught his eye at the time because it was dark, unlike every other decoration in the place ... and now he knows it wasn't a decoration at all.

Marie knows it too. "Mr. Rialto told me about that damn box," she says after Lonnie and Vito tell their stories. "He told me what he used it for too. It's no wonder Lonnie and Vito and their pals hated his guts."

While Charlie runs to Petrilli's to pick up the box, Peg the Coroner takes another look at the fragments of Dominick's blown-apart skull. The new examination reveals signs of additional trauma that occurred before the gunshot. Pine splinters and plexiglass shards are embedded in the sites of that trauma.

When Charlie gets back with the box, Peg finds it has a splintered edge matching the pre-gunshot contusions in Dominick's cranial shards. Also, though someone scrubbed down the box recently, there's still a bloody fingerprint on it. It just so happens Peg's able to match that print to the very guy identified by Vito and Lonnie as the fourth conspirator. He might appear to be an upstanding citizen, but his prints are on file thanks to a DUI arrest a few years back.

"Let's go grab the S.O.B. before he hightails it." Burt looks at Marie. "You comin' along to close the deal?"

"I wouldn't miss it. I owe my old informant that much." Marie checks her watch. "But then there's no way I'll make it to Midnight Mass in the 'Burgh as planned."

"You'll miss your solo." Charlie thinks for a moment, then pulls out his phone. "But maybe I can do something about that, if you're interested. I think *I* can open some doors for *you*."

Dr. Eugene Savino the chiropractor is just locking up when Charlie, Burt, and Marie arrive at his office in downtown Abruzzi. Cherubic as he is—a little guy with thin black hair, chubby cheeks, and an elfin nose—he doesn't look happy to see them. He knows Charlie and Burt, but his body language makes it clear he's not in the mood to have a conversation with them.

"Merry Christmas, guys." He turns the key in the lock. "Whatever you want, it'll have to wait till after New Year's."

"Actually," says Charlie, "we just need a tube of that Bionumb lotion. I'm fresh out, and your place is the only one in town that sells it."

"Love to, but I'm on my way home," says Savino. "Then I'm going on vacation."

"Oh, God." Burt grimaces and releases a moan of the deepest anguish. "I can't stand it! Oh, please, make it stop!"

"Poor guy." Charlie, looking concerned, puts a hand lightly on his shoulder. "Bionumb's the only thing that helps him, and we're all out."

"You mean I have to *feel* like this the whole way through the *holidays?*" Again,

Burt moans like he's about to drop dead on the spot.

Savino blows out a disgusted breath, then turns the key back the other way and opens the door. "All right, one tube. Wait here."

When he enters, Charlie and Burt don't wait as instructed. Instead, they follow him inside. "I can't thank you enough for doing this," says Charlie. "He's really in a lot of pain."

"Police work's *killin'* my spine!" Burt says with a wince.

Savino hurries behind the counter, grabs a short white tube with blue lettering from a bin on the wall—then puts it back and pulls out a longer one. "Here. It's on the house." He throws it to Burt. "Happy holidays."

"Doc, you're a lifesaver," says Burt. "I mean *back*-saver."

"Dominick was right about you." Charlie nods. "He said you were a stand-up guy."

That gets Savino's attention ... but he chooses to brush it off. "Well, I have to get going, detectives." He lingers behind the counter, smiling. "Christmas Eve awaits."

"Not for Dominick, though." Burt chuckles. "That poor goombah."

"Mr. Rialto, you mean?" Savino plays dumb. "Has something happened to him?"

"You tell us," says Charlie.

Savino casually drops his hands to the edge of the counter. "There's nothing to tell. He's a patient of mine, but ..."

"That's not *all* he was, though, right?" Charlie's hands are at his sides, relaxed. "We found out a few things during our investigation, actually."

"I still can't believe he ripped you off the way he did." Burt laughs and shakes his head. "I mean, you're a *doctor* ..."

"Well, a *chiropractor*," corrects Charlie.

"You're a *smart guy*, is what I'm sayin', and he still tricked you with that dumb *gadget* of his," says Burt. "Tricked those other guys too—Tony Petrilli, Lonnie DeGol, Vito Arcurio ..."

"Lots of other folks, as well," says Charlie. "And it was such a *simple* trick. There were three colored lights on a box in the trunk of his car—one green, one amber, one red. He'd flip a switch, and they'd go on and off, one at a time. You'd bet which one would still be lit at the end when he flipped the switch off. It was sort of like picking where the pea ends up in a shell game. *Except ...*" Charlie smiles. "*Except* it was *rigged*. Dominick had a guy under the back seat, and he heard what color you called, and then he always made sure a *different* color came up at the end."

"Pretty sneaky," says Burt.

"Pretty profitable, for Dominick," says Charlie. "There's just one thing I can't figure out. How could a smart guy keep placing bets on something like that? Wouldn't he catch on that it's rigged?"

"I guess they probably let you win just enough, huh? Made you think you could win it *all* back." Burt nods knowingly.

"Happens to the best of us," says Charlie. "You're not the first moron to get taken, and you won't be the last."

"Is that why you helped kill him?" asks Burt. "We know because you left traces of Bionumb on his neck, and this is the only place in town that sells it."

Savino's gaze is like a lizard's now, coolly flicking from one of them to the other. He's thinking things over, weighing his options—and then his upper arms twitch.

Which is exactly when Charlie explodes. "*Don't you move, asshole! Hands where we can see them!*"

Defiant, Savino keeps his fingers on the counter, ready to drop fast and grab the gun he keeps under there.

"You heard him!" Burt whips a Glock .22 from the pocket of his parka and swings it up to aim at the chiropractor. "Whatever you're thinking of trying, don't do it!"

"Take a look out front," says Charlie. "You get past us, you still have *her* waiting for you."

Savino looks out the front window, and Marie stares back from behind the barrel of a .45.

"They gave you up, dumbass." Burt snickers. "Your co-killers Tony, Lonnie, and Vito."

"Lonnie and Vito had a falling out," says Charlie. "Vito was *shooting* at Lonnie when we found them. It didn't take much to tip them over the edge."

"Once *they* threw you under the bus, Tony wasn't far behind," adds Burt. "Why wouldn't he be? You might be Italian, but you ain't *la famiglia* like the rest of 'em."

"It was the *list* that showed us the way," explains Charlie. "We thought at first it was some kind of mob Christmas list—but then we realized it's a *checklist* for a *murder*. A checklist Dominick must've torn out of one of your pockets even as you four pricks murdered him.

"Tony's on the list for a hundred tabs of OxyContin. We know now that was the gift you four used to get Dominick to invite you into his home.

"Lonnie supplied the guns and ammo to kill Dominick ... though wasn't that a little *overkill* after you bashed his head in with the light box?

"Vito brought a Persian rug to roll the body up in, and you brought a Cadillac

Escalade to transport dead Dominick to Central Park. Killing him at his home wasn't enough, apparently."

Burt snorts. "*You* had to put the body on *display* in the *park*. You really wanted to drive the point home that the guy got what was comin' to him."

Savino looks like he's finally starting to sweat. "You can't prove *any* of that."

"We've got three confessions," says Charlie. "Plus, we lifted a print from the light box. Surprise, it's one of yours."

"We've got C.S.I.s combing Dominick's house for the actual murder scene, and we'll find that too," says Burt. "We'll find the blood evidence, because you can *never* completely clean that shit up. Face it, smart guy, you're goin' down."

"So what'll it be?" asks Charlie. "Live to crack backs another day behind bars? Or get your final adjustment the hard way?"

Savino stands there, considering. Then, with a sigh, he steps back from the counter and raises his arms.

"Good choice, Dr. S.," says Charlie. "I guess you're a wise man, after all."

It's five past midnight when the lights go down in St. Gregory's Catholic Church, but the place isn't dark at all. Every parishioner in the packed house holds a flickering candle as the priest—Father Gus, a friend of Charlie's—reads the story of the Christ child.

Charlie, sitting in the middle of the crowd, isn't Catholic, but he appreciates the atmosphere. He gets a shiver up his spine as he gazes at the crowd of worshippers and the decorations around them. The marble altar at the front of the church is surrounded by poinsettias, and the huge cross hanging above it is draped with a long white stole. A Christmas tree laden with liturgical ornaments glows at the head of the left wing of the transept; the head of the right wing features a life-size Nativity scene, complete with a golden star glowing overhead.

It's not what Charlie's used to, but he doesn't mind. He's done his best to help Marie, and he can't wait to see how it all works out.

Since she couldn't make it back to her home parish in Pittsburgh in time, Charlie called Father Gus and talked him into finding a spot for her at St. Gregory's that night. Given that Marie's a total pro, and the priest at her church in the 'Burgh sang her praises to Gus over the phone, getting her on the bill was no problem at all. As for the 'Burgh church, a quality stand-in was available and glad for the chance to cover for Marie.

All is right with the world, therefore, which is as it should be on Christmas Eve.

Marie's happy, and Charlie's happy he could help her. All that's left is for the lady to sing her heart out.

As Charlie watches, the choir files in, dressed in white robes trimmed with gold. Marie is the last to enter, looking more radiant than ever.

Charlie can't stop smiling as the choir sings "Hark! The Herald Angels Sing." He can't take his eyes off Marie, who looks like a perfect angel with her dark hair flowing over her white-robed shoulders.

When she sings her solo, the chills are back big-time. Charlie doubts she can see him in the candlelit shadows, but he likes to think she's singing only for him anyway.

She's singing for him on Christmas Eve, with another case in the win column, one that both of them had a hand in solving. The evidence is clear: they make a great team.

So what if she lives two hours away in Pittsburgh? There isn't a doubt in Charlie's mind that he's going to ask her out on Xmas Day. The only X-factor is whether or not she'll say yes.

Though that's kind of a gift itself, isn't it? Because guys like him just love a good mystery.

NOT EVEN THE MOUSE

A You-Solve-It by Eric B. Ruark

Sheriff Tracy Hyers pulled her patrol car up in front of one of the homes that faced the bay down by the abandoned factory. The house was weather beaten and had seen better days. Deputy Sheriff Winston Gates was standing at the door.

"You are not going to believe this one," he said as she walked up to him. Deputy Sheriff Gates was ten years older and a hundred pounds heavier. He had to stand out of the way to let her pass.

He opened the door for Tracy and directed her to the kitchen in the back of the house where Vicky Edison was sitting at the small table holding a baby in her lap.

After the usual cute baby pleasantries, Tracy asked, "Why don't you tell me what happened?"

"Someone broke into my house last night," Vicky said.

"What did they take?" Tracy asked.

"Nothing," Vicky said. "Come look." She stood up and carried the baby into the small living room.

Sheriff Hyers looked around. The room was small and kind of dingy. Baby toys were scattered everywhere and there was a small, wooden play yard with mesh sides sitting next to a sofa chair that faced a small screen flat TV. To the right of the chair was a small, artificial Christmas Tree with several brightly wrapped presents tucked underneath.

Vicky pointed to the tree and presents. "Look. They are not mine," she said.

"What?" Sheriff Hyers responded.

"They are not mine," Vicky said. "Whoever broke in here left the tree and the presents for me and my son."

"Yeah, we have to arrest Santa Claus," Deputy Sheriff Gates said with a barely hidden smirk.

Tracy gave Gates a look that made him leave the room. "Make yourself useful and look for a point of entry," Sheriff Hyers called after him.

"When did you discover the break in?" Tracy asked Vicky.

"This morning when the baby woke me up and I came out to heat up his formula.

I have to walk right past the living room and there they were."

"You didn't hear anything?" Sheriff Hyers asked.

"No. Bobby and I sleep in the same room. I'm usually a light sleeper because of the baby. Last night he woke me up. He was laughing and saying something about a mouse or as he says it, 'mouth, mouth.' I gave him a stuffed toy and then went back to sleep. When I woke up this morning, the presents and the tree was there."

"Didn't you have a tree of your own?" Tracy asked.

"No," Vicky answered. "Things are a bit tight right now and I figured that Bobby is so young, he won't know he missed this Christmas."

"Who knew that things were tough for you?" Tracy asked.

"Just about everyone that knows me," Vicky said. "I have a job, but the hours aren't great, and I have to balance how much I make at work with the Day Care costs."

Deputy Sheriff Gates came back from looking outside. "No sign of break in," he said. As he stepped into the living room, the floor squeaked.

"Do you leave a key or something outside?" Tracy asked.

"Yes. I keep a spare in a key safe under a rock outside," Vicky answered.

"Who knows that?" Tracy asked.

"Well, there is my next-door neighbor, Mrs. Higgins, and my boss, Mr. Falks. Mrs. Higgins baby sits for me on occasion and Mr. Falks gave me a ride home one night and he had to open the door for me because my arms were full."

Sheriff Hyers walked past her deputy and went outside to check on the key in the key safe. It was still there. Then she walked down the street to Mrs. Higgins house and knocked on the door. An older woman with long gray hair answered the door.

"May I help you?" the older woman asked.

"Are you Mrs. Higgins?" Tracy asked.

"Yes. Is there something wrong?"

"There was a break in next door last night and I was wondering if you heard or saw anything?"

"A break in? How awful? What could anyone take from that poor girl?"

"That's just it. They didn't take anything. Instead, they left presents for your neighbor and her child. You don't happen to know anything about that, do you?"

"No, I don't, but that's a wonderful story. She is such a good kid. She deserves some of the season's blessings."

After talking with Mrs. Higgins and ruling her out as a suspect, Tracy drove over to where Vicky worked. The manager, Mr. Falks was in.

"I'm shocked, absolutely shocked that anyone would break in on that young woman. She works so hard to provide for her son. I would give her more hours, but the economy being what it is."

Mr. Falks shook his head. He was a heavy-set man in his fifties.

"You didn't happen to leave those presents?" Tracy asked.

"Do I look like Santa Claus?" Mr. Falks asked.

"I don't know," Tracy responded. "What does Santa look like?"

Back at the Sheriff's office, Tracy sat down at her desk. Deputy Gates walked up to her. "What are you going to do about the break in?"

"Do I look like the Grinch to you?" Tracy asked.

"You mean you know who left the presents?"

"Of course. Don't you. You solved the crime."

WHO WAS VICKY'S SECRET SANTA?

Solution in next month's issue ...

SOLUTION TO NOVEMBER'S YOU-SOLVE-IT

A Cozy Arrangement By John H. Dromey

Miss Hennessey followed the policeman outside and shared her suspicions with him. "I'm convinced Millicent Brubaker was murdered. Ask yourself a simple question. Without actually seeing it in place, how could Flo reasonably deduce the candy was uneaten? She's the likely killer and she must have peeked into Millie's room before the body was discovered by Julie. I've told you the *who*, but you'll want additional proof. A thorough autopsy should reveal the *how*."

Detective Rodriguez returned a few days later with an arrest warrant for Florence Porter.

Privately, the detective explained the official theory of the case to Julie. "Sometime before injecting her rival with a lethal amount of insulin, Flo substituted carob for the real chocolate you'd placed in Millicent's bedroom. After one bite, Millie declined to eat the rest of the candy, thereby suggesting a presumptive time and cause of death, plus—if everything went according to plan—eliminating her killer's need for a credible alibi. Fortunately, Fluffy arrived on the scene just in time to prove otherwise."